FOLLOW POPPY

WRAITH

CASSANDRA DOON

Have you ever read a classic and thought... what if this was spicy...

Copyright © 2024 by Cassandra Doon and Wraith

All rights reserved.

No part of this publication may be reproduced, distributed, or transmitted in any form or by any means, including photocopying, recording, or other electronic or mechanical methods, without the prior written permission of the publisher, except in the case of brief quotations embodied or critical articles or reviews. For permission requests, contact doon.co@hotmail.com.

This is a work of fiction. Names, characters, places, and incidents either are the product of the author's imagination or are used fictitiously. Any resemblance to actual persons, living or dead, events, or locales is entirely coincidental.

Independently published by Cassandra Doon and Wraith

Edited by Taliah

First Published December 2024

Edition 2

Cover design by Best Selling book Cover

Interior design by Vellum

Author Website: Cassandradoon.com

PROLOGUE
OFFICER WILLIAM "WILL" ANDREWS

The night air is crisp, settling over the slumbering town like a shroud. I let it fill my lungs as I patrol the empty streets, the silence punctuated only by the soft hum of the cruiser's engine. There's a stillness to this place after dusk, which seems almost sacred, but tonight it feels... different. My fingers tighten around the steering wheel, and I can't shake this sense of foreboding that gnaws at my insides. It's the feeling that precedes calamity, the calm before a storm I can't yet see.

I've driven these Louisiana roads more times than I can count and watched over the people of Transylvania for years, but the weight of responsibility never lessens; it rests on my shoulders, as heavy as the gun secured at my hip. This vast nothingness of scattered houses and buildings surrounded by bare fields and marshy lands by the Mississippi River is a dent in the world. The population of almost no one as we seem to be the preferred pickings of the shadows that go bump in the night.

With each passing second, the quiet eats away at me, a

reminder of all those unresolved cases that haunt my dreams, specters of guilt, and what-ifs that linger in the corners of my mind. Whatever causes such carnage yet leaves no trace? A cop's worst nightmare, body upon body and bloodless damn all to go by. I detest not being able to piece together what happened to these unfortunate souls so I can end it occurring yet again.

A sudden movement catches my eye, a stark, jarring contrast against the motionless backdrop. My heart stutters, then races as I pull up alongside the figure materializing from the fog of my headlights. It's a child, no more than four. Her tiny form seems impossibly fragile and at odds with the asphalt sea that engulfs her. Blood... God, there's so much blood coating her clothes, staining her hands, and smearing across her cherubic face. It's a tableau that screams wrongness, painting a picture of horrors unseen.

I vacate the cruiser but leave the driver's door off the latch as I approach the little girl. My movements are deliberate and slow because scaring her is the last thing she needs.

"Hey, sweetheart," I say, my voice gentle despite the adrenaline singing through my veins. I crouch down to be more at her tiny level, my arms resting on my knees. She stares up at me with wide, glassy eyes, and something about her gaze pierces straight through the armor I've built around myself. It's a look that begs for safety, for answers I'm not sure I can give.

Without warning, the night erupts into an orchestra of dread; there's this distant rustling of leaves as a whispering wind carries echoes of secrets best left buried. The darkness around us seems to close in, as though the very shadows are alive with malice, conspiring to swallow any trace of innocence left in this world. My pulse thunders in my ears, a drumbeat of primal instinct urging me to shield this child from the unseen threats that lurk beyond our pool of light.

"Who did this to you?" I ask, though, the question tastes of betrayal, hinting at trust shattered, and sanctity violated. There's a story written in the crimson that covers her, a tale of danger that I'll unravel thread by bloody thread if it's the last thing I do.

For now, I decide the best thing to do is give her comfort in this gruesome bad dream. I scoop her into my arms, her small body trembling against my chest, and I vow silently to stand as her guardian against the encroaching night, against whatever malevolent force has cast its shadow over my once peaceful town.

I stand up straight and go to the car, seeking to get us away from the dreadful crime beyond the cypress trees veiled by dense sheets of Spanish moss. "Can you at least tell me your name, little girl?" My voice is barely audible, a futile attempt to bridge the gap between her unfathomable experience and my helplessness.

"Poppy," she murmurs, the single word a fragile shard of identity amidst the chaos. Her tiny hand, smeared with a crimson testament to her ordeal, trembles as it rises, pointing with unmistakable intent toward the heavy grove of trees that cling to the faraway hill's edge like a shroud, past the bog before us. There, where the moonlight dares not linger, lies the silhouette of an abandoned manor that gives the illusion of a castle from the old country, its crumbling spires casting long shadows that whisper of forgotten tales and forsaken promises.

The silence stretches taut, ready to snap under the weight of unspoken fears. The wind carries a chill that seeps into my bones, foretelling of perils hidden within those timeworn walls.

2 weeks later…

I STAND ALONE in the fading light of dusk, the amber horizon bleeding into shades of deep purple as night asserts its dominion. The wind whispers through the desolate streets of our small town, carrying with it the scent of rotten eggs from the swamp and a chill that settles not just in the bones but deep within the soul.

I've scoured every corner and knocked on every door that might hold the key to unraveling this dark enigma. Yet, it feels as if I'm chasing shadows grasping at the wisps of a dream just beyond the brink of daybreak.

Despite an extensive search, Poppy's parents remain untraceable, seemingly scrubbed from reality with unsettling thoroughness. It's a silence that resonates louder than thunder, a void where there should be life, laughter, and answers. It's as if they had vanished into the ether, so utterly complete is their absence, leaving behind only the haunting question of why. The vacancy sign they've left tugs at me, a constant reminder of my duty and the fear that some stones are better left unturned. But I can't; I won't allow myself that luxury. Little Poppy deserves more.

As darkness falls like a sheet over the world, my senses sharpen, prickling with the urgency of the hunt. Shadows lengthen into grotesque shapes, each a specter of doubt and suspicion that clings to the fringes of my resolve. Somewhere out there, beneath the indifferent gaze of a million stars, lies a truth so carefully concealed that it mocks the very notion of justice. Every rustle in the underbrush, every soft sucking sound of sunken feet in the wet ground, heightens the sense of a lurking presence unseen yet palpably malevolent.

The midnight's breath grows thick with the stench of decay, a tangible manifestation of the rot that festers unseen within the heart of this mystery. Mine comes in short, measured bursts, fogging the air as I push forward, driven by adrenaline and dread. This case has burrowed into my marrow, a parasite feeding on my peace of mind, whispering insidious doubts that erode the bedrock of my convictions. What if the betrayal runs deeper than I dared to imagine? What if those entrusted to protect have become the architects of deception?

Every step feels like a descent into a labyrinth where the Minotaur is not a beast of flesh and horn but one of lies and half-truths, its labyrinthine passages constructed from human frailties and dark secrets. I can't shake the feeling that danger lies in wait just slightly farther past my flashlight's reach, watching, waiting, biding its time until I stumble into its web. And yet, the greater peril is not to the body but to the soul, for the abyss I gaze into threatens to gaze also into me, to consume me with its insatiable hunger for oblivion.

ONE

POPPY AGE 8

The world seems to shrink, collapsing in upon itself like some dying star, as I am whisked away from the only fragments of a past I can claim. They tell me my parents are gone, reduced to phantoms haunting the edges of my fractured memory.

The nice man with piercing blue eyes and dark brown hair graying at the roots found me roaming around, drenched in blood as the folktale goes, the deserted roads of this small ghost town that is Transylvania, Louisiana; Officer William Andrews, I think it was, never came back to see me, not once. He promised me he would find out the grim truth behind my tragic beginnings, that he wouldn't rest until he did. Promises broken, like myself. Another sheep plucked from the flock; I overheard the grown-ups from the children's home I was at whisper amongst themselves. He chased shadows, only to be consumed by them, as they say.

A disrupted narrative with too many blank pages, that's what I am. Now adrift in a system that churns relentlessly like the gears of an indifferent clockwork universe. With each passing day, week, month, and year, the faces blur, the names fade, and I become little more than a specter wafting through temporary homes and fleeting connections.

They call me Poppy, a name snatched from thin air by someone who decided it suited the girl with the enigmatic yellow-colored eyes and the quiet demeanor. The foster system is a purgatory for lost souls like mine, each seeking a harbor against the storm. Yet within this storm of uncertainty, there's a whisper of hope piggybacking on the wind, a pledge that refuses to be extinguished despite the relentless assault of doubt.

Then, after four years of this endless void, like a sudden break in the gloomy clouds revealing the benevolent face of the moon, they arrive. A couple from the big city, their presence like a warm hearth fire in the depths of winter. Arthur and Isabella Hartwood introduce themselves, their voices tinged with a longing that mirrors my heart's emptiness. Their eyes speak volumes, heavy with tales of silent rooms and unfulfilled dreams. They extend their hands, not just in greeting, but as an offering, a lifeline cast into the turbulent sea of my existence.

"Poppy," Arthur says, his voice steady and reassuring, "we'd like you to come live with us, to be a part of our family." The word 'family' hangs in the air, a beacon in the gathering darkness, its profound and terrifying meaning. Can a word so simple bridge the chasm of loneliness that yawns within me? "What do you say?"

"Ok." What else can I say but that?

The Hartwood are the stark opposite of me. While I

look pretty much like Snow White, with porcelain white skin, black as a raven's feather hair, crimson red lips, and unusual yellow eyes, they are dark-skinned with dark brown eyes and hair. We won't fool anyone, but that's not the point. Sometimes, family is who you choose it to be. Sometimes, family runs thicker than blood.

Hand in hand with these strangers, I forsake the shadows that dance in the corner of my eyes and my mind. The ones that recede from view the moment I do my utmost to look closer. A hide and seek game I can't ever win because I don't know the rules to it yet.

It pains me to leave the place that holds my blackened past, but I can't be stuck in this nightmare forever, in the main, when there's nothing I can do about it. Perhaps, when I am older, I can return and fill in the gaps of the many cracks in my story. For the time being, a normal existence doesn't sound so bad.

We journey 248 miles to New Orleans, the Big Easy, and the Crescent City. It seems far, but what if it isn't far enough?

As I step across the threshold of their white picket fence home in the beautiful Garden District, I can't help but feel the ghosts of my unknown past clawing at my heels, eager to drag me back into the abyss. Whatever I sought to leave behind followed me, it seems.

The house is a fortress against the encroaching night. Still, even within these walls, I sense the pervasive tendrils of an evil force lurking in the depths of my subconscious. It's as if opening their hearts to me has painted a target upon us all, inviting dangers I cannot see per se but feel with every fiber of my being. Maybe normal is not something a basket case like me can be.

I shiver, not from the cold but from the realization that acceptance comes with its price. In embracing this new life, have I inadvertently exposed my new guardians to the spectral threats that hound my every step? The thought is a splinter in the grey matter of my brain, oozing with the poison of guilt and fear.

Amid the turmoil, Arthur's hand rests gently on my shoulder, a silent vow of protection that bolsters my faltering spirit. When I look up at him, desperately seeking a bite of faith that screams this wasn't a deadly mistake, he peers down at me with a small, confronting smile.

"We're here for you, Poppy," Isabella whispers from my other side, her words wrapping around me like a protective shroud. "Nothing can harm you now. I promise." I can sense their resolve, fortified by love and an unspoken oath to shield me from the storm that rages unseen. But the last time someone gave me their word against these ghosts, they rested six feet under torment.

As night falls and the house settles into a deceptive peace, I find myself peering into the darkness, searching for the eyes I know are watching, waiting to reclaim the enigma that is, from this moment on, Poppy Elise Hartwood.

TWO

AGE 21

I stand at the precipice of reality, where the tangible world frays into the tapestry of dreams. A decaying mansion, abandoned and veiled in the whispers of time, casts a shadow that stretches towards me like an accusation, or is it an invitation? The air is thick with nostalgia, a scent that never truly belonged to me yet clings to my soul with the tenacity of a preordained destiny. My heart, a captive bird within its bony cage, flutters with anticipation as I behold the grandeur of ruin before me.

"Poppy," murmurs the wind, or perhaps the crumbling stone itself speaks. Shadows, formless yet sentient, emerge from the mansion's darkened maw. Three of them merge into silhouettes that dance upon the edge of perception. They reach out with tendrils of darkness, each whispering a siren's call, luring me closer to the abyss that claims to be my birthright.

"Come home," they breathe, their voices a chorus of longing and despair intertwined. "You belong with us."

The dream fractures, shards of illusion slicing through the veil as I jolt awake. My bedroom, starkly contrasting to the haunting splendor of the dreamt castle-like structure, greets me with its familiarity. Sweat clings to my skin, a cold reminder of the chasm between worlds. I survey my sanctuary, my gaze falling upon the desk where papers lay, printed and pristine, detailing the lease of the mansion that haunts my slumber.

For one week, those documents promised an answer to the riddle that is my existence. The phantom manor, an enigma etched into my very being, calls to me in dreams and now through the binding words of legal agreement. What secrets does it hold? What truths will it reveal about the blood-stained child found walking that small Louisiana town so many years ago?

The hush of Transylvania envelops me as if I am submerged in a memory deep and still. Its silence is not peaceful but heavy with untold stories, the deserted streets whispering tales of days long forgotten. I see myself anew, smaller, fragile, but a specter against the backdrop of desolation, my tiny frame drenched in crimson that seeps into the cobblestones like a sinister stain. The eerie atmosphere clings to me, a cloak woven from the chill of unanswered questions and the weight of an unknown past.

I recall how Officer Andrews - yes, I still remember his name - found me, a child abandoned, my innocence marred by the blood that painted my skin and clothes, an indelible mark that time has never quite erased. The towns-folk spoke in hushed tones, their eyes wide with fear and pity. The mansion loomed over us all beyond the trench line of the Mississippi River, its shadow stretching like fingers across my life, shaping it with its dark embrace. Even now, years removed from that fateful day, the feeling of being out of place, of belonging to another world, courses me both a comfort and a curse.

My phone pings from under my pillow with a constant string of messages, breaking the trance as abruptly as it arrived. With a shuddering breath, I pull myself back to the present. I guess the gang has awoken.

ROSIE:

Oh my God, witch, today is the day we break the cherry of your past.

LUKE:

Morning to you, too, Rosie.

BEN:

Please remind me again why we need to leave so early. It's the crack of dawn, everyone.

HENRY:

Aww, does Princess Ben need his beauty sleep?

BEN:

Fuck off, loser.

· · ·

ROSIE:

Boys behave.

Henry darling, you know Ben is a cranky bastard before caffeine.

Don't poke the bear.

I CAN'T SAY I had a lot of friends growing up. I was marked by a sad, soppy story outcast with strange, unusual yellow eyes that no one wanted to get close to in fear of me dragging their poor, unfortunate souls to the deepest parts of hell. I never sought to try to get out of my solitude and fabricate bonds with the other kids.

It wasn't until university that I was assigned Rosie Blackwood as my roommate, and something changed. The pretty girl with light olive skin, green eyes, and shoulder-length chestnut hair, which was more often than not tied back in a practical ponytail, saw the havoc that is Poppy Elise Hartwood. Instead of pushing me away and running in the opposite direction, she pulled me closer.

"Us lost souls gotta stick together. Maybe that way we can find our way somewhere." Rosie told me once upon a time.

After she came to the boys, the bad boy duo Dean, his younger brother Samuel, or Sam for short, sweet nerd Oliver, and the playful jocks Henry, Luke, and Ben. One by one, they found their way into my black heart and melted the resolve to stay hollowed up by myself, forever alone, amongst the shadows that haunt me. Just like that, many mismatched misfits became the people I cherish the most, apart from my dear adoptive parents, who had been the only speck of light in my life thus far.

The odds are that the more people someone like me cares about, the more blood will spill, saturate, and stain my hands in the end. They are bound to get hurt as something vicious and treacherous seems to have taken heed of me, sank their sharp claws deep, and marked me as theirs. I was grudging, letting them all come along on this trip down a murky memory lane.

"The Scooby gang doesn't consist of one person, Pops. You can't face your past alone. Who will root you to the present if we are not there for you? No. Either we all go, or you aren't going either. Sorry, not sorry." Luke had very forbiddingly informed me.

So here we are now, all early rising to the genesis of something that might have dire consequences.

POPPY:

Morning everyone.
Where's Dean and Oliver?

DEAN:

Here, catwoman

DEAN GREYSON. Tousled dark brown hair with piercing pale blue eyes, fair skin, about 6 feet, a slender frame but with lickable abs. He has a tattoo of a moth in black and white in the center of his chest, with some more ink scattered around his flesh. According to the bible, this alluring winged parasite represents the decay of a person's life.

The first time we met, he almost ran me over on his ZR10R motorcycle. Instead of apologizing, he raised the visor on his helmet. He winked at me before making the beauty between his legs howl and driving off into the metaphorical sunset. Things have been simmering between us ever since.

He told me my yellow eyes reminded him of those of cats, so 'Catwoman' became his pet name for me. I don't mind it. It's cute.

OLIVER:
Present

OLIVER THOMPSON'S medium-length hair desperately needs a trim; always chaotic, which I am grateful for as it gives me a reason to brush my fingers through it. Meadow green eyes that look at the fucked up world with as much curiosity as my own eyes. Freckles stain his cheeks and nose, which marries nicely with his pale complexion. He's as tall as Dean and has pretty much the same build.

He and I are quite close, seeing that we are quite similar. He is quiet, somewhat bashful when amongst people we don't know and don't care to get to know, and reserved when it comes to our past stories. I would put Oliver on the best friend pedestal alongside Rosie, even though sometimes I wonder if we could be more.

. . .

SAM:

Wow, good to know I mean nothing to you, Dahlia

AND THEN THERE'S the other Greyson. At 6 '4", he was slightly taller than his brother, with the same color hair and eyes. He was lean but a bit more muscular than Dean. Sam is one year younger than us, making him the baby of the group. But don't tell him that to his face; he hates being reminded of it.

I don't think Samuel Greyson likes me very much, but Rosie opposes it; she believes he might have a crush on me. He calls me by other flower names except for the one that is my name.

Flinging my legs over the side of the bed, the echo of those voices calling me 'home' still rings in my ears, but they are quieter now, thanks to my friends. The room is dimly lit by the dawn's early light, casting long shadows across the floor that seem to reach for me, beckoning. As I stand, every movement feels deliberate, charged with the urgency of one who knows that each step taken is one closer to an inevitable confrontation.

As the remnants of sleep dissipate, replaced by a fore-boding sense of urgency, I can't help but wonder if the answers I seek are worth the price I may have to pay. The shadows' invitation lingers in my mind. Is it a seductive trap or a genuine plea for my return? Amidst the echoes of betrayal that seem to resonate from the manor's hollow heart, I must decide whether to embrace the darkness or flee it again.

THREE

TODAY

"I double-checked the supplies, Poppy," Rosie murmurs, her voice tinged with the thrill of impending discovery. And Lucas has confirmed he's bringing his camera gear, as requested." I nod, my heart thrumming with an exhilarating and disturbing energy. In the echo of our preparations, there's a symphony of excitement and the undercurrent of a question: What awaits us within those forsaken walls?

She and Henry were the first ones here, and we set off packing the car with all the stuff we deemed necessary for the trip. Seeing that this is Henry's car, half of the supplies in the trunk are snacks. We are just now awaiting the rest of the gang's arrival with the second car.

These two have been together for the first year. They are that annoying couple that every group of friends has, and they are all lovey-dovey with each other. Cute but cringeworthy sometimes. I get kicked out of my and Rosie's dorm room more times than I can count, thanks to all the rolling around in the hay; that's what she calls them to do. Luckily, Dean's couch is always free in his and Sam's trailer and on the outskirts of the big easy. That or I end up in Oliver's dorm watching investigative docuseries on his laptop.

"Life is too short. You should follow your heart when it ushers you to someone or someplace." An extremely in-love young woman spoke Rosie's many words of wisdom.

Henry Caldwell is the archetype for the pretty boy next door. He has sandy blonde hair and bright Nordic blue eyes, and he plays basketball alongside Luke and Ben for our university's team, so he's pretty fit. Rosie is the captain of our track team, which means she is very athletic, too. Bitch can run fast. Meanwhile, you have me, who hides in the dark corner of the library by herself or with Oliver, nose-deep in a book. Dean and his all-black ZR10R; if he's not in class or hanging with us, he is in the garage where he works playing with his baby. And Sam, God only knows what his thing is, probably hating me.

"They are here." Rosie didn't have to point that out; you could hear Dean's motorcycle coming from a mile away. That machine's purr is loud.

"I thought you weren't bringing your baby with you?" I ask when he stops right in front of me in the driveway behind Henry's car, while Sam parks his 1962 pale yellow Chevrolet C10 by the street curb to the fore of my parents' house. Oh, that explains the bike. The truck fits three people in the front seat, and that's about it. "What happens to Ben's car?"

"Wouldn't start. I tried everything. The way I see it, Benny boy killed his alternator with the stupid ass amplifier he decided to put in the trunk." Dean observes after taking his helmet and mask off, swiftly grazing his fingers through his disheveled hair, somehow making it even messier.

"You didn't tell me the alternator might've been too old; how should I have known, dude?" Ben remarks once he's out of the truck with Sam and Luke on his tail.

"That's what happens when you do shit yourself. We have a mechanic in our midst; you should've just let Dean do it." Henry says, his arm draped over Rosie's shoulders.

"Too late now." Ben, our dirty blonde-haired boy with old-world blue eyes, mumbles under his breath.

"I will fix it when we get back, bro. Hey, Catwoman, you think your parents would mind if I leave Batsy in your garage?" Dean asks me.

"Of course not. Go right ahead." I tell him.

"Dude, I can't believe you named your bike Batsy." Luke, the ash brown-haired boy with hazel eyes, comments. "Weirdo."

Dean had dismounted from his baby and was dragging it to the already open garage door. Still, at our dear friend's words, he halted, lifted one of his middle fingers, and shouted, "Shut it or suck it. Dick." Boys, I think to myself, rolling my eyes.

"Petunia," Sam says as he takes his usual stance of hands buried deep in his jean front pockets, looming over me like he always does.

"Samuel," I reply, staring back at his pale blue eyes.

"Right. Everyone is here; everything is set," Rosie declares, her dark green eyes alight with fierce determination and her words with a slight urge to defuse the obvious tension between me and the younger Greyson, "let's get this show on the road."

My friends are rallied, the route plotted, and the unknown beckons with its siren call. We are ready, or so we tell ourselves. I ride with Sam and Dean while the other five get in Henry's car. The only thing pulsating in the truck is the soft hum of Samuel's favorite band, Paragon of Virtue's Inferno, until my phone vibrates in my hand.

ROSIE:

Hello from the other side.

POPPY:

You are such a dork.

I don't see a thousand missed calls on my phone, though.

ROSIE:

She lives

POPPY:

Barely.

ROSIE:

Oh no, what have the Greyson brothers' done?

· · ·

POPPY:

Nothing.
I just never heard silence quite this loud.

DEAN HAS BEEN GAZING out the window, watching the world rush by, his head resting on his palm, which in turn is perched on the window sill, as his other hand draws tantalizing circles with its fingertips on my upper thigh. In the meantime, Sam is either looking out the windshield angrily as he drives us to our final destination or peering at me, actually, for the most part, where his brother's palm lies on my leg, with the same pissed-off look.

ROSIE:

Do you at least have Church's voice to keep you company?

POPPY:

The only saving grace.

"THE GLARE from your phone is too distracting, Petunia." Sam remarks.

"The way you glare at me is intrusive too, your point being?" I tell him with the same irk he threw my way. "Also, you already used that flower name today. Did you run out of blossoms to call me?" I ask as I glance at him.

"Kids behave. Or I will coop you two up somewhere

until you make out." Dean threatens us, which is brushed aside since you can hear the teasing behind it.

"I think you meant to say 'made up,' idiot," Samuel informs his brother.

When I look at Dean, his pale blue eyes gravitate to mine, and he winks at me as a corrupted smirk pops up in his gorgeous face. "I said what I said, brother." I frown at his statement. What is he up to? What is he cooking up in his reckless yet beautiful mind?

After what feels like forever, our convoy of headlights finally pierces the twilight as we draw near the imposing silhouette dominating the horizon. The phantom manor looms before us, its castle-like spires clawing at the darkening sky, a reminder of a time when such towers were not just dwellings but bastions against nightmares made flesh.

"Fuck me dead, Petunia, this place it's out of the gorges of an Edgar Allan Poe poem?" Sam comments.

The cars come to a gravelly halt, and we all step out, our breaths visible in the crisp air. The mansion's exterior is a tapestry of gothic splendor and decay. Sad, pallid Gargoyles leer from their perches, eyes empty yet watchful, and ivy clings to weathered stone like the desperate embrace of the forgotten.

A shiver courses through me as I gaze at the highest tower, where shadows play tricks upon my sight. Could it be the settling dusk or something more sinister watching from those hollow windows? The weight of countless secrets seems to press against this place's ancient rusty black gates. As they groan open at our approach, I can't shake the feeling that we are stepping into a web woven long before our arrival. A web of danger, deceit, and the echoes of betrayal that cling to these stones like a curse.

The air tastes of dust, and a foreboding settles in my chest. This mansion, a specter from my fragmented memories, holds the key to understanding who or what I am. But with each step forward, the sense of urgency mounts, and the darkness around us thickens as if the evening warns us of the threshold we dare to cross.

The chill of the evening creeps through my bones as I stand momentarily rooted to the gravel path. Beside me, Rosie's breath fogs in the air, her wide eyes reflecting a cocktail of exhilaration and unease. "This is insane, Pop, " she utters in a hush tone.

The manor's gardens sprawl before us like the remnants of a dream, untamed and whispering long buried tales. Wild blood-red roses strangle the skeletal remains of trellises, and thorns seem to reach out as if beckoning us closer. The silence here is profound, broken only by the occasional rustle of leaves, suggesting the presence of something unseen.

Why does it feel like I am home?

FOUR

"Feels like we've stepped through time," Luke murmurs, his voice barely above a whisper, as if afraid to disturb the tranquility.

I nod, unable to form words, captivated by how the overgrowth clings to the stone statues, rendering them grotesque guardians of a bygone era. There's a beauty in the decay, a sad song that resonates with the deepest chambers of my heart. A longing for an understanding I can't quite grasp settles within me. A yearning for answers hidden beneath the ivy and the moss.

As I ponder the entwined histories these grounds must hold, a shadow detaches itself from the darkened entrance of this phantom manor. The figure of Liliana Ravenshadow, our enigmatic hostess, glides toward us with an otherworldly grace that belies human nature. Her silver hair cascades over the shoulders of her dark gown, a river of moonlight against the encroaching night. Her sage green eyes, unnervingly still, lock onto mine as though she perceives the tumult of my soul.

"Welcome," she intones, her voice a melody that threads through the thickening fog, "to my humble abode." Each word she speaks is deliberate, heavy with an import that suggests layers of meaning yet to be unveiled.

Rosie shifts beside me, her hand clasping mine, a silent testament to the magnetic pull of Liliana's presence. Our hostess's gaze does not waver; it drinks in our essence, understands our fears, and promises revelations that may forever alter the fabric of our reality. I glimpse a labyrinthine depth in her eyes, a well of profound knowledge that borders on the abyssal. With a single glance, she has unraveled us, leaving us exposed and vulnerable before the arcane truths this castle-like erection harbors.

"Thank you for allowing us to be here, ma'am." Dean, ever the charmer, utters to the mistress of the house.

"Shall we?" Liliana gestures toward the yawning darkness behind her, an invitation laced with urgency and the unspoken assurance of danger that lurks within those ancient walls. It is not a question but a summons, one we are powerless to resist. As we move to follow her lead, I feel the weight of history pressing down upon us, a tangible shroud woven from the threads of countless untold stories. We are walking a path paved with betrayal and cloaked in shadows, where every step might bring us closer to enlightenment or trap us in the jaws of a forgotten tragedy.

Liliana Ravenshadow beckons us into the belly of her dark stone mansion with a cryptic smile that barely disturbs the solemnity of her expression. The massive doors groan an ancient lament as they part to reveal the grandeur of the entrance hall. I step over the threshold, and it is akin to crossing into another realm, where time has relinquished its relentless march. The air within is redolent with the musk of buried epochs, and my breath mingles with the dust of centuries.

"Holy crap, look at this place," Benny says as he spins around, looking up at the resplendence of it all.

Towering ceilings vault overhead, adorned with intricate frescoes that speak of a former sumptuousness now shrouded in the cobwebs of neglect. Arches loom, carved with the visages of stern ancestors who watch over this domain with eyes that have witnessed the inevitable decay of their bloodline. Gargoyles leer from shadowed alcoves; their grotesque features a silent testimony to the hubris that once filled these halls. Each step on the mosaic floor echoes a resonant dirge that mourns the lost splendor of this place.

Liliana's silver mane cascades like a moonlit waterfall as she glides ahead, a specter of grace amidst the ruins of glory. "This mansion," she announces, her voice a melody that weaves through the melancholy air, "has stood sentinel for centuries, guarding secrets that many would seek and few should find." Her words are riddles wrapped in the velvet of her enigmatic charm, compelling yet leaving the heart uneasy.

"Wow, she's a character, hmmm?" Sam comes up behind me and whispers down my ear. I peer at him, tossing the younger Greyson a frown that screams, 'Don't ruin this for me.'

He chuckles. "Relax, Lavender. I didn't mean it in a bad way, geez."

"Why can't you be more like your brother?" I ask him,

revolving my face so I am looking ahead and away from him

"You mean a suck-up?"

"Nice. Charming." I throw at him.

"Every story needs a foe."

"And you want to be mine."

"At least that way, I am part of your dark tale." And with that, Sam vanishes from my personal space. I seriously don't get that, boy.

"What's his problem?" Oliver asks me the second he joins me at my side.

"Who knows, curly? But if you find out before me, please tell me." I answer as I loop my arm around his.

In the drawing room, time itself seems to falter, held captive by the faded splendor that surrounds us. Antique furniture, with its silhouettes softened by the passage of years, stands as a warden of the past. Portraits of aristocrats hang upon the walls, their expressions tinged with the melancholy of a dying lineage. Every brushstroke of the hauntingly beautiful artwork whispers tales of grand balls and whispered conspiracies, of love kindled. Judas kisses wrought in the flickering candlelight.

"Each piece," Liliana says in a hushed tone, gesturing to a tapestry frayed at the edges, "tells a story, a fragment of the areas of our history." Her eyes, those piercing sage green pools that seem to glimpse at your soul, fix upon each of us in turn, imparting the weight of suppressed narratives that yearn to be heard. She speaks of lords and ladies whose laughter once filled these rooms, now replaced by an oppressive silence that bears down upon my chest, heavy with the ghosts of yesteryears.

I feel the fabric of my reality fraying, unraveling thread by thread as we tread deeper into the mansion's embrace, of old opulence tarnished by the patina of age, its faded majesty a stark reminder of the impermanence of power, the fleeting nature of human endeavor.

"Hey, Catwoman, you doing alright?" Dean asks me, draping his arm over my shoulder as we tread on the heels of the lady of the house.

I reach over with my hand so I can hold the one that is dangling from my shoulder. I squeeze it before telling him, "All good, batman. Just taking everything in. It's a lot." He nods in acknowledgement.

As we meander through the shadowed labyrinth of corridors, I am acutely aware of this place's breath. This slow, ponderous exhalation seems to carry with it the howls of conversations of way back when. Liliana pauses before an unassuming stretch of wall, her slender fingers tracing an invisible pattern in the air. With a faint click, a section of the stone pivots inward, revealing a narrow passage draped in cobwebs and secrecy.

"Damn, now that's what I am talking about. That's so bloody cool." Ben comments.

"Secrets upon secrets," she declares. A shiver runs up my spine, not from the draft that snakes its way out from the dark maw before us but from the realization that this fortress is much more than mere stone and mortar. My companions exchange glances, eyes wide with wonder and trepidation as if the very walls beckon us to peel back the veneer of reality and peep at the raw sinews of history beneath.

We saunter softly over creaking floorboards that groan

under the weight of our modernity as if complaining about the intrusion. The air grows thick with the scent of old parchment and dried roses, carrying with it the echo of footsteps not our own. It is as though the mansion itself remembers those who once walked its halls and, in remembering, calls out to them across the chasm of time.

A bouquet of awe gasps echoes all around me. In one dimly lit chamber, away from the world's prying eyes, I spot what has caught my friends' attention. A painting that arrests my gaze and ensnares my soul the moment I lay eyes upon it.

"She's beautiful," Samuel states, lost in wonder.

A woman, garbed in a gown of raven feathers, stands amidst a stormy sea, her hands reaching towards a sky painted with the anguish of thunderheads. Her visage is sublime sorrow, eyes like amber flames flickering with secrets and loss. And though her features are unfamiliar, something in the curve of her lips, the arch of her brow, strikes a chord within me, a haunting melody that resonates with the hidden corners of my fragmented memory.

"Poppy," Liliana's voice cuts through my reverie, sharp as a knife's edge, "does it speak to you?"

"It does," more than I care to admit. The painting is a siren call, a beacon from the depths of a past I cannot recall yet cannot escape. The brush strokes, laden with foreboding, seem to dance and shift with a life of their own, whispering of breaches of faith and trust so profound it has bled into the canvas, staining it with the ink of long-ago treachery.

The mood shifts, the air charged with urgency as the

darkness appears to press closer around us. There is danger here, palpable and hungry, lurking in the silence between one heartbeat and the next. I feel it in the marrow of my bones, the sense that the woman in the portrait knows me, that her sorrow mirrors my unremembered grief.

"Be wary," Liliana warns, her words barely above a murmur, yet every syllable is laced with an intensity that sets my nerves on edge. "Some portraits are windows to the soul, others doorways to damnation." Her cryptic observation hangs suspended in the dank and stuffy air while the woman hanging up on the wall seems to plead with me, her eyes imploring me to uncover the truth hidden within her storm. But am I ready to weather the gale of revelations that awaits? Or will I be swept away, lost to the storm of whispers and shadows that cling to these ancient stones?

FIVE

"Poppy, look." Drawn from the painting's spectral embrace, I turn my head to follow Oliver's gaze as it flits across the grand hall's opulent decay to a staircase that coils upward like a slumbering serpent made of stone. "Shall we see what secrets lie above?" he inquires, his voice a beacon of adventure amidst the shadows that cling to the phantom manor's heart.

Liliana regards us with a mysterious smile, the corners of her mouth twitching with unshared knowledge. She nods once, silently granting us passage into realms untold.

The staircase before us rises majestically, each step a testament to ancient splendor. It is a spiral of ascendancy that wraps around its axis as if chasing the tales spun within its architecture.

"Watch your step." Liliana intones, her voice a melody woven from the dusk air itself. "These steps have borne the weight of history and speak to those who listen."

"Ominous much," Sam utters from behind me. I halt

on my steps, making him collide with me, his arm going around my middle to keep us both from falling.

I peer at him, giving the younger Greyson a death stare. "Don't be rude."

"What? It's not my fault the lady out of a gothic nightmare is saying a bunch of stuff without really saying anything at all."

"Mrs Ravenshadow has kindly allowed us in her home, she can as easily kick us out. I need this, Sam."

"Fine. Just don't look at me like that, Snapdragon, you know it only makes me want to piss you off more."

I roll my eyes at his last comment. "You, Samuel Greyson, are a man-child, I swear."

I place my hand upon the railing, feeling the chill of carved marble seep into my skin, and break away from Sam's hold. It is a cold whisper from the past, an echo of the countless souls who have traversed this path before me. As we ascend, the air shifts, growing denser with the dust of ages and the breath of secrets long since whispered. With each step, a shiver travels up my spine as if the very stones recognize the tread of an ancient kinship. My heartbeat syncs to the rhythm of our climb, the pulse of anticipation that throbs through the veins of the mansion.

A murmur, soft yet insistent, begins to caress my ears. A susurrus of voices entwines with the creaking protest of each stair underfoot.

"Can y'all hear them?" Rosie murmurs, her eyes alight with the thrill of the unknown. "The whispers are getting louder." It seems these walls can talk.

The air grows colder still, wrapping around us like an unwelcome shroud. Each breath we exhale gives birth to ghosts swirling in the chilling silence, mingling with the hushed voices that seem to seep from the wall. The closer we get to the unseen summit, the more pronounced they become, a symphony of soft, low-spoken tones that tell tales of sorrow and betrayal, of dark deeds veiled in the shadow of time.

A knot forms in my stomach, coiling tighter with the ascent. What awaits us above? What truths do these ancient stones yearn to divulge? My mind races with possibilities, each more unsettling than the last, as we continue our journey skyward. The atmosphere thickens, pregnant with the promise of revelations that may well turn our blood to ice.

"Almost there, children," Liliana assures us, her voice now laced with an urgency that mirrors the pounding in my chest. Yet, even as we ascend, I cannot shake the feeling that something ascends with us, an unseen presence that watches from the darkness, waiting to claim whatever secrets we unearth.

"Damn, this thing goes on forever," Henry remarks when we crest the final step, soon followed by a deadly silence falling over us. I am unsure if he meant the stairs or the corridor that stretches ahead now, its walls lined with candles that flicker like the last breaths of the dying. Their feeble glow casts shadows that dance macabre waltzes across the stone, teasing my imagination with forms that are not entirely human.

"This is insane," Luke comments.

Oliver hums next to me. "What is it?" I ask him.

"This place doesn't belong here." That's all he says. I swallow hard, trying to steady my racing heart. The air here is thick with history, each flame illuminating centuries of secrets etched into the cold, unyielding surfaces.

"Watch your step." Liliana's lyrical voice caresses the stillness, a gentle reminder of her presence guiding us through this realm of whispers and watchful darkness.

"Does anyone else feel like they are being watched?" Dean asks, his eyes darting to every dark corner.

The sense of being observed is palpable, as if the walls have eyes that follow our every move. A shiver runs down my spine, an involuntary tribute to the unseen observers who silently witness our intrusion. I am but a trespasser among these ancient echoes, my soul resonating with the melancholy of forgotten tales and lost souls eternally bound to this forsaken place.

"Look there." Liliana gestures with a slender hand to a heavy door that stands ajar, its dark maw promising secrets untold.

With measured steps, we cross the threshold, and suddenly, the oppressive atmosphere yields a vastness that takes my breath away. Moonlight streams through grand windows, bathing the room in an ethereal silver. The view before us is haunting beauty, a tapestry of moonlit gardens and shadowed groves stretching far into the distance until they merge with the ink-black sky. "Exquisite, isn't it?" Liliana's voice barely rises above a whisper, yet it slices through the silence with the precision of a blade.

The stone mansion's grounds sprawl beneath us, an isolated kingdom cloaked in night's embrace. I can see the gnarled limbs of ancient trees, their twisted silhouettes standing over the undulating landscape. A lone tower's spire piercing the heavens reminds me of the isolation that envelops this place. It is a beauty born of desolation, a reminder that splendor often wears a veil of sorrow.

"Mind the edges," Liliana warns, her tone urgent, intense, "many have been betrayed by the false promise of security within these walls." Her words hang in the air, mingling with the chill that creeps into my bones.

My eyes land on Sam, and I am sure a crude remark is about to part from his lips, but nothing ever comes. His hands are buried deep in his jeans' front pockets while he stares, frowning intensely at Liliana and biting his lower lip. He must have felt my eyes on him because he met mine. That's when he winks at me, and an evil smirk appears. See, man, child.

"You have no faith in him, Catwoman."

"Nope," I tell Dean.

The older Greyson chuckles. "At least he kept his mouth quiet this time."

There is danger here, lurking in the gloom, a darkness deeper than the absence of light. It is a peril that whispers of betrayal, of treachery sewn into the very fabric of this mansion, an evil force that watches, waits, and hunger for those who dare to uncover its secrets.

As the whisper of the wind caresses the night, I stand motionless, my gaze tracing the contours of the moonlit domain below. The vastness of the manor's grounds, bathed in an ethereal glow, holds a sorrowful beauty that resonates deep within me. It is as if each shadowy grove and silent turret harbors a piece of my fragmented past, a silent witness to the secrets I am yet to unveil.

Beside me, the others are mere silhouettes, lost in their

contemplations, but Liliana captures my attention. Our eyes lock in a moment stretched by the gravity of unvoiced recognition. There is a depth to Liliana's piercing green stare that seems almost otherworldly, an abyss that promises both knowledge and oblivion. My breath catches; in her gaze, I sense a kinship with the unknown, a shared lineage with the arcane. She stands between worlds, her presence a bridge to the untold stories etched into the manor's stone. And though her lips remain still, her eyes whisper tales of forgotten times, beckoning me to listen, to understand.

"Poppy," Liliana finally speaks, her voice a soft echo against the stones, "there is much for you to discover." I nod, unable to tear my gaze away, feeling the weight of destiny pressing upon my shoulders. She knows more than she lets on, much more, and I sense that she will be the key to unraveling the mysteries that have haunted me since childhood.

The silence stretches, laden with meaning, until… a sudden chill brushes my neck, and the hairs on my arms stand on end. From the depths of the haunted mansion, a sound disrupts the quiet, a low, mournful howl that swells and fades like the lament of a ghostly choir. The others stir, unease rippling through them, but I stand rooted, transfixed by the haunting cry.

"Did you hear that?" Rosie's voice trembles, barely above a whisper.

"Stay close," Liliana commands, her calm demeanor belied by the swift glance she casts over her shoulder. We exchange glances, our collective curiosity now tinged with fear. The howl rises again, closer this time, a symphony of despair that sends shivers down my spine. It beckons us, pulling at the very fabric of our resolve. "Come," Liliana urges, her silhouette a dark promise against the candle-light, "we mustn't linger here."

But as we turn to follow, something flickers in the periphery of my vision, a fleeting glimpse of movement, a shadow detaching itself from the darkness. I pause, heart pounding, wondering if the secrets of this manor are coming alive to claim us or reveal themselves.

"Poppy?" Rosie's hand finds mine, her fingers cold with dread.

"Something's here," I whisper, staring into the gloom, where the unknown waits with bated breath.

SIX

T he lingering scent of ancient dust and the subtle chill of hidden secrets envelop me as Rosie, and I recline in the grandeur of the drawing room. I can't say I know where the boys ended up, though. They are probably still exploring this phantom manor's never-ending corridors and rooms.

Navigating this labyrinth with Liliana has left me with a tapestry of emotions. I am pleased with the discovery, yet an undercurrent of unease threads through my excitement. The enigma that is Liliana Ravenshadow occupies my thoughts, her aura resonating with the same mysterious allure as the stone walls that encase us.

"Can you believe the history etched into every crevice of this place?" Rosie muses, her dark green eyes wide with the reflection of firelight and wonder. "Liliana... she's like a character from one of those old gothic novels, isn't she?"

I nod, my mind adrift in the sea of uncertainty that her presence evokes. "There's a story behind her eyes," I say, more to myself than to Rosie. "A tale woven with strands of shadow and light, but she guards it as fiercely as the mansion itself."

"Perhaps we'll unravel some of it during our stay," Rosie replies, her words tainted with hope, as she bumps her shoulder to mine.

The door creaks open as if summoned by our conversation, casting an elongated shadow across the weathered floorboards. Liliana glides into the room, with the boys following her in, as she bears a tray laden with an ornate teapot and baskets filled with what promises to be a late-evening snack. She moves with a grace that belies the heaviness of her burden, setting it down upon the coffee table with a precision that seems rehearsed or perhaps ritualistic.

"Tea will warm you through the night ahead," Liliana remarks as she sits on the antique Victorian walnut sofa facing ours. Oliver sits next to me as Henry does so at Rosie's feet; Luke and Ben fan around the lady of the house while the Greyson brothers stand next to the fireplace.

I am so grateful this bunch of misfits is here with me. Don't get me wrong; I don't mind the loneliness, but I crave belonging, and these seven messed-up wonders make me feel like I do.

While my past is a blank page stained with blood, theirs is a hard-to-forget nightmare. With a faceless and nameless father and a mother who had to get all dolled up, Rosie hands out love all night to pay the bills with no clothes on. The Greyson brothers, their druggie parents, and the hide-and-seek game the boys used to play with social services, all so the two of them wouldn't end up separated. Oliver and his overbearing parents shaped all of his anxiety and depression that compelled him to cut his flesh more often than not. Ben, with a bible belt upbringing that was shoved down his throat by his holier-than-thou parents, who couldn't love who he wanted for fear of punishment, so he stayed locked in a closet. Luke, with a drunk father, was more of a dead weight than his very sickly mother. Still, he needed him around because, thanks to his veteran-free health care, Lume was able to pay for his mother's hospital bills and pills. And then there's Henry, probably the better off in terms of money; despite that, he had an emotionally distant mother and a narcissistic, abusive father who was trying to live his scattered basketball dream because of a torn anterior cruciate ligament through his son. University was their ticket to a new beginning, a way to heal from their traumas. This is mine.

The flickering flames from the fire cast a macabre dance upon the walls, their shadows reaching out like spectral fingers as they played upon Liliana's gaunt features, making them even sharper. Her piercing green eyes lock onto my peculiar yellow ones, and I'm trapped by the intensity within them, a silent warning echoing in the depths of her gaze.

"Be wary," she intones, the urgency in her voice sending a shiver down my spine, "these walls whisper truths and lie in equal measure; trust not the specters of the past that roam these corridors."

Rosie shifts uneasily beside me, her hand finding mine in search of solace. My heart races and every beat is a drum, sounding the march toward an unknown fate. We are pawns in a game played across the checkered floor of this mansion, a game whose rules Liliana knows but divulges only in riddles.

"Remember, the brightness of day cannot unveil all that hides in the night's embrace." Her cryptic counsel is tangible and heavy, with the weight of unspoken threats lurking just beyond our sight.

I swallow hard, the taste of fear sour on my tongue. The manor's secrets are a living entity, pulsing within its walls, entwined with the legacy of betrayal and blood. What have we stepped into? And can we ever hope to step out again?

"Once I depart," Liliana's words slice through the thickening air. It would be best if you secured the main entrance. The mansion is yours to discover, but venture not beyond its protective enclosure." Her gaze holds mine, an unspoken covenant passing between us. These walls are your sanctuary and cell; do not forsake their shelter."

Oliver leans forward, his curiosity, a living thing that cannot be caged by fear or warning. "But what creeps outside that we should fear so deeply?" He asks.

"Many things." Liliana answers, cryptic as ever. I hate to admit it, but I am starting to understand Samuel's exasperation with the tall, slender lady with long silver hair cascading down her back. "Some draped in the guise of friendliness, others less veiled in their hunger. You must not invite them in." I feel a chill, colder than the draft whispering through the cracks of this old mansion, seep into my bones, almost as if a presence has made itself known. "Promise me," she insists, eyes searching ours for understanding, "that you will heed my warning."

"We promise," we say in unison, though the word tastes like ash upon my lips. A vow made in the shadows of the unknown is nothing but an empty promise. Curiosity is a killer, after all.

"Deny entry to all who may call," she reiterates, her tone sharpening into something urgent and insistent. It is not merely a request; it is for your survival."

My heart hammers against my chest; each beat echoing the perils that might prowl at the manor's threshold. Rosie's hand grips mine pretty tightly now. From now on, we are bound by more than friendship; a pact sealed with Liliana's foreboding counsel is our hangman's noose. Let's see if we listen; if not, we might choke ourselves with it or snap our necks if the fall is high.

"What about this place that has you so spooked, Ma'am?" Dean asks.

"Long before these stones were erected," she begins, her voice a haunting song luring us into the cavernous dark depths of its history, "these grounds were whispered to be kissed by the otherworldly. The veil between realms, gossamer-thin and trembling with ancient magics."

Oliver leans forward, his curiosity showing again, a bright flame amidst the gathering gloom. "What sort of magic?" He asks in an almost feather-light manner.

Liliana's lips curve, not quite a smile, more a knowing arch. "The kind that ensnares the heart and ensorcells the mind. Guardians have been appointed through the ages, their lives woven into the stones you tread upon. They serve as protectors and jailers to forces that hunger for release."

I swallow hard, the weight of her implications settling

upon my chest like the tomb's slab. There is a majesty in the way she speaks of the manor's past and an unmistakable thread of caution that weaves through her tales. It is as if the air breathes with the pulse of untold stories, each a specter awaiting discovery.

"Tell us more about these guardians." I implore, the thirst for knowledge grappling with the ice of fear in my veins.

"Ah, dear child," Liliana sighs, her gaze drifting toward the fire as though it might conjure images from the ashes, "their sagas are etched in the silence of these halls, felt rather than heard. But beware, for even stone can betray, and echoes of the past may yet reverberate with consequences unforeseen."

With a grace that belies the gravity of her departure, Liliana rises, her form a silhouette against the hearth's glow. With each step toward the door, the atmosphere tightens, a coil ready to snap. Her hand hovers over the doorknob, pale against the dark wood. "I shall return in seven days. Keep the doors locked, children, and trust in the protection they afford."

The door closes with a click that resounds like a final note in a symphony of warnings. The sound seals us within these ancient walls, a silent benediction, or perhaps a curse, left in the wake of her retreat.

SEVEN

"I 'll be back in seven days." Liliana's voice, now distant, carries a gravity that tethers my soul to the floorboards. Shadows lengthen, conspiring with the encroaching night as we rest rooted to our spots, stranded in a sea of uncertainty, surrounded by the whispers of a mansion that houses more than just ghosts.

"What is this? The ring?" Ben asks with indignation. "Boo. Seven days." The dirty blonde boy comments that last bit, mimicking an eerie specter.

"Isn't that spoken as an omen of the characters' death after they watched the tape?" Dean asks.

"I think Mrs. Ravenshadow said seven days 'cause that's how long we rented this place for, you idiot," Rosie observes.

"For all one knows, laying eyes or even stepping foot on this haunted mansion could act like the tape, and we secured our tragic fate that way." Sam blurs out. Silence falls as his words sink in.

"Let's not let the evening's ominous tone detain our

spirits," I murmur with a voice that seems foreign in its attempt to ward off the chill of fear.

"Ominous hmmm, Dandelion?" Sam notes.

I pay no heed to the younger Greyson's taunt, hurriedly declaring, "This mansion is ours to discover, and we've barely scratched the surface of its mysteries." The words feel hollow, yet they carve a path through the inertia that had claimed us.

"Can we scratch it in the morning? I am tired. All I want to do is eat the goodies Liliana brought us and then find a room to crash." Luke announces.

"If Henry decides to leave some scraps for the rest of us, sure," Ben remarks, tossing a dirty look on Henry's way.

We all stare at the boy who has been gorging on the little sandwiches and pastries our dear hostess has graced us with. The guy eats like he has a hole or a worm in his guts.

"What?" Henry asks with his mouth full.

"Sharing is caring, dude." The older Greyson tells Henry, his black leather jacket squeaking as he crosses his arms under his chest.

Rosie giggles as Luke says, "You better be ready to live by the words you preach, my friend." Dean gazes at the ash-brown-haired boy, one of his eyebrows arching. I reckon he's at a loss about what that statement meant.

"Luke." I retort in warning because he and Rosie are the only ones who know my heart's darkest appetite, but that's my truth to confess, not his.

"Sorry, sorry, just ignore me." He utters, lifting his hands in surrender.

This takes me back to the drunken night a few weeks ago when we were outside Greyson's trailer staring up at the stars while the others were inside playing silly video games. My back was against the trailer's wall, legs spread flat, with Rosie mirroring my pose, facing me, her back to the wooden fence that makes up the slowly rotting porch we were sitting upon. Luke was lying down, his head on my lap, as I brushed my fingers through his brown strands.

Out of nowhere, Rosie declared to Luke that he and Benny would make such a cute couple. Luke's cheeks blushed, but his smile was wistful. The thing about those two is that they unquestionably like each other. While Luke is open about his feelings, Ben is letting the tainted and prejudiced society, with its old-fashioned concept of right and wrong, control who they can love. Or maybe it's just his parents' religious poison that still flows in his veins.

"You guys are letting other people dictate your happiness. Fuck that; you should just go for it; judgment be damn." I'd set forth.

To which Luke replied, "I ain't. It's hard for Ben, you know that. And how hypocritical of you, my dark bloom, since you, in a way, are holding back too."

"It's different though. My heart is greedy; it tells me I need three." Or maybe I am unquestioningly guided by the faceless shadows in my somber fantasies.

"Is that why you are not letting Dean date the shit out of you? You can start by telling him that and finally permit him to take you for a ride." I chuckled at Luke's comment because he didn't mean in the older Greyson's motorcycle. "Seriously, Pops," he continued, "you can cut the sexual tension between you two with a knife. Something's got to give. Oh, and while you are at it, maybe give poor Oli a chance; the dork only has eyes for you."

"Luke." I tried to intervene.

"And Sam." My fellow flower-named friend jumped into the conversation.

"Samuel? I am sure he would much rather die a slow, agonizing death than date me. Or screw me."

"Hate fucks, are the best kind of fucks."

Shrugging off mine and Luke's spoken words, Rosie uttered, "What's more romantic than a beautiful castle-like manor up in a hill buried amongst the cypress trees draped in a Spanish moss shawl? Those stone walls are already embedded with tales of love and loss; what's two more? You two should just come clean to the ones you all want."

My yellow eyes met Luke's hazel ones; written in their depths was hope that undesired consequences don't come and bite us in the ass. Stuff like this can ruin friendships.

Dean's hand finds mine, his touch an anchor amidst the storm of doubt that threatens to sweep me away, and it steers me from my adrift thoughts. I find myself looking out the batterbee-decorated floor-to-ceiling windows, but all I can see beyond the glass is pitch black. When did the night become this consumed by darkness? And when did I get up from the antique Victorian sofa I was sitting upon?

A Victorian Gothic style shrouds every inch of this phantom manor, blending elegance, luxury, and dark drama. Most walls are either adorned with somber floral and damask print wallpapers or soberly painted in a bold black, which sadly is now stained with white patches from old damps. The furniture, flooring, and even paneling are done in dark hardwoods like mahogany and walnut, with beautiful intricate carvings. Fabrics seem to be velvets, brocades, and lace; the ivory of the sheer net curtain finds itself at odds with the hues of moody maroon, smoky amethyst, cool slate, and ashy teal. Luxurious, ornate chandeliers, majestic stone fireplaces, and stunning candle holders with decaying white tapers cast a soft glow to this mansion's many rooms. How gloomy, yet enchanting.

"Found you," Dean tells me. His fingers interlaced with mine are a silent promise of shared adventure or perhaps shared folly.

"Was I lost?" I ask him, our eyes coming together.

With a playful glint that belies the gravity of Liliana's cautionary tales, he leans in close, his breath a warm whisper against the coolness of my ear. "Let's find a room." He says, his lips grazing my earlobe in a tender, teasing caress.

A shudder courses through me, a visceral response that tightens my core with an anticipation that feels almost forbidden within these walls. "Sure," the word escapes me, a soft surrender to the pull of desire that Dean so effortlessly invokes. I look beyond the older Greyson and notice it is just me and him. "Where did everyone go?"

"Hunting for their bedchambers, my lady. Shall we?" He asks. I nod in agreement, giving him a shy smile.

Our connection, this unspoken understanding that thrums between us become my guiding light as we leave the drawing room to explore the shadowed corridors, our hearts beating a rhythm that drowns out the whispers of the past.

Time to come clean and maybe get a little dirty.

EIGHT

T he manor's somber atmosphere wraps around me like a shroud, its silence oppressive, yet there's a calling within it, a voiceless echo from the deep recesses of my memories.

"Where are we going?" Dean's voice ripples through the stillness, tinged with a hint of his usual humor. Still, I can detect the undercurrent of concern for me for this journey into my past. He might've been the one who pulled me from the drawing room, but the moment we stepped into this maze of endless corridors, I was the one stringing him along somewhere.

"Something feels... familiar," I murmur, more to myself than to him, as I brush my fingers along the cold surface of the wall. The faded thread weavings and ghostly statues seem to watch us pass, guardians of history lost to time and my fragmented recollection. "Like a half-remembered dream teasing at the edge of waking thought."

Dean's hand still holds mine. His touch is warm and grounding, yet my heart aches with the weight of unanswered questions of a life once lived within these walls, now reduced to mere whispers in my mind.

Our shared breaths create foggy halos in the frigid air as we press on, the pull of destiny or perhaps just raw curiosity guiding our steps until we arrive at a doorway that seems to sigh open, inviting us into its secret embrace.

"Cause that's not creepy at all." The older Greyson remarks at the door before us, just swinging open on silent hinges and surrendering to an unseen creature's unspoken command.

"Something's waiting for us." I breathe out, my hand tightening around Dean's as we prepare to face whatever remnants of the past linger hungrily in the room that calls to me with the voice of a siren, sweet and terrifying all at once.

A sliver of light cuts through the darkness, casting an ominous glow that beckons us with silent urgency. My pulse races, each beat screaming a warning as I inch closer to the threshold, drawn by a force I cannot name nor fully comprehend. Shadows flicker at the edges of my vision, their forms indistinct and menacing, as if the very essence of the night has come alive to trap us in its web.

"Poppy, be careful." Dean's voice is a low growl laced with protectiveness. His body is tense beside me as though ready to act at the slightest hint of danger.

The soft golden illumination within the room seems to pulse, a beacon amidst the encroaching tenebrosity that seeks to claim every corner of this forsaken place. My nostrils fill with the musty scent of old leather and rosewater's faint, sweet trace.

"Can you feel it?" I whisper, the words barely escaping my lips as a tremor courses through my body. The room beyond is not just a space; it is a sentinel of secrets, a holder of horrors that once danced gleefully in the minds of those who dared to dwell within its confines. I step across the threshold; my footsteps muffled by the plush carpet that swallows sound and seems to cradle my every move; each step forward is like a battle. The door creaks a death toll that echoes in the cavernous hollows of my soul. What lies beyond is both salvation and damnation, a test of wills between the allure of the unknown and the primal instinct to flee.

The room unfolds before us like a scene from an ancient tapestry, alive with the flickering glow of candle-light that casts an ethereal luminescence upon the chamber's hidden corners. Dark silhouettes dance across the high-backed chairs and lavish draperies, a spectral ballet choreographed by the quivering flames. Every object speaks of a grandeur that once was in this place forgotten by time, now muted by the relentless march of days.

"Poppy." Something within the dwell breathes out my name. A strange serenity descends upon me, a cloak woven from the air that fills this space, as the room resonates with whispers of a past I can almost touch yet remains veiled in the deep recesses of my mind. My heart, a captured bird within its cage, flutters against the confines of my chest, yearning for the secrets that linger just beyond reach. How peculiar it is to find solace in a place so steeped in memories not quite my own, a refuge that feels like home despite the years that separate me from whatever life once stirred within these walls.

"Did you hear that?" I asked the boy, who willingly followed me in.

"Do you mean the deafening silence? Yeah, I guess I can hear it." Dean answers.

The air grows heavier as I advance; each breath I draw is now laden with the scent of aged wood and wax, the fragrance of antiquity itself, mingling with the coppery taint of something unsettling. It clings to the gilded frames of portraits whose eyes follow me with an intensity that belies their frozen expressions. There is beauty here, but it is tinged with melancholy, a reminder of the transient nature of all things. I am caught in the liminal space between now and then, my soul echoing with the sorrow of loss and the hope of rediscovery.

I pause, allowing the moment to envelop me, letting the silence speak its long-dead language. What tales could these walls tell if only they had voices? Would they sing of joyous feasts and laughter ringing through the hall, or would they whisper of quiet sobs muffled by thick damask, of hearts breaking in the absence of light? The past is a puzzle, and I am a piece adrift, searching for the place where I belong.

The candles burn lower, their light dimming as if weary from their long vigil. Shadows stretch longer, bolder now as if encouraged by the consuming darkness. Somewhere in the distance, the phantom manor groans, a lamentation of stone and wood, a sound that seems to come from everywhere and nowhere. It is a reminder that despite the tranquility that wraps around me, there is an undercurrent of unrest and disquiet, a sense that something unseen moves beyond the periphery of vision. My pulse quickens, my senses sharpened by the primal instinct to flee the invisible threat that slithers through the ill-lit, hopeless limbo. Yet, even as fear pricks at the edges of my consciousness, I cannot deny the pull of this place, the allure of its enigmatic heart. In a room that knows my name, danger, and discovery intertwine like two threads in the same tapestry, impossible to unravel without tearing the fabric of my being.

I feel the weight of countless untold stories pressing down upon me, the chill of obscured eyes tracing the curve of my spine. Once a haven, the chamber begins to warp, its warm embrace tightening into a grip that hints at desperation, almost suffocating, at secrets too long buried. The dance of darkened silhouettes grows frenzied, a macabre twist of shapes that beckons me to look closer, to see what lurks in the bold interplay of light and dark.

Dean pulls me to him, making my back crash to his front. His touch is gentle yet burdened with unspoken questions. He spins me around to face him, and I am met with the depth of his piercing blue eyes, a turbulent sea that threatens to pull me under. In their reflection, I see the shadows of my doubts mirrored back at me.

The dying flickering glow of the candles casts a halo around him, giving him a beautiful angelic allusion. "Poppy," he begins, his voice a soft rumble against the room's stillness, "are you still with me?"

"Yeah," I tell him quietly, my yellow eyes swaying between his blue eyes and lips.

"So I haven't lost you to this place yet?" I shake my head as I bestow Dean with a soft-hearted little grin. "Good. Poppy," he clears his throat before continuing, "I need to know... what do you think about my proposal? Can you imagine a future tethered by commitment, or does the very thought constrict your wild heart?" His words hang between us, delicate and fraught with meaning. I search his gaze, finding a longing for connection that resonates within the caverns of my solitude. Be that as it may, there is more to me than one man's embrace can encircle, more than a whisper in the dark can call forth. I am a soul untamed, a spirit that thrives in the presence of manifold affections. Deep down, Dean knows that.

Here goes nothing. I will either break us with what I am about to set forth or bind us together this midnight. "Commitment," I utter, tasting both promise and cage, "Dean, I am drawn to you more than you could know. But my heart beats to a rhythm composed by many hands, not just one." The confession spills from me, a river breaking its banks. "I yearn for ties that branch out like the roots of an ancient tree, deep, intertwined, and reaching in all directions."

The following silence is heavy, charged with the electricity of truths laid bare. The shadows peek from the spots they skulk by and stretch across the room, crawling along the walls and creeping towards us as if drawn to the gravity of our discourse. My breath quickens as the air thickens with anticipation and the scent of burning wax.

"Multiple partners?" Dean's question cuts through the hush, sharp and clear yet tinged with an edge that borders on something dangerous. "Is that the kind of freedom your soul seeks, Catwoman?" The weight of his question is palpable, a challenge issued amidst the rising tide of unease that floods the chamber we find ourselves in. I stand firm, my resolve steeling me against the burgeoning storm.

"Yes," I affirm, my voice a beacon in the gloom. "To love and be loved in return, by more than one, without bounds or barriers. That is the dream that whispers to me in the night."

NINE

ean's sigh ripples through the tenebrous space between us, a sound that seems to carry the weight of a thousand unspoken words. He tilts his head, the shadows cast by the flickering candles playing upon the sharp angles of his face, revealing a swamp of emotions that dance in the depths of his guarded blue eyes.

"Perhaps," he begins, his voice a low murmur that resonates within the walls of my fractured memories, "there is a path that winds through this bayou of feelings, one where you can wander freely. I could... I could let you explore, experience... others." His proposal hangs in the air, a delicate offering wrapped in vulnerability and the faint hope of understanding.

My heart flutters, like a bird trapped within the cage of my ribs, as I consider the labyrinthine corridors of my desires. The idea of being tethered to one while yearning for the stars has always felt akin to wearing a gown of thorns, exquisite yet excruciating. Dean's suggestion is a key offered with trembling hands, the promise of a door swinging open to reveal a lush and untamed garden of possibilities.

"Freedom," I whisper, tasting the word on my lips, "with you still at my side?" It is not merely a question but a horizon beckoning me toward the dawn of a new familiarity.

A mischievous smile unfurls across my lips, a silent rebellion against the chains of conventionality. I reach up, my fingers brushing against the stubble that lines his jaw before descending, a trail of sparks igniting with every touch until they find the warmth that emanates from his jeans. My hand rests there, bold and unapologetic, as I lean in closer, our breaths mingling in the charged space that pulses with each beat of our hearts.

"I would love that," I confess, my voice barely above a hushed tone, imbued with layers of longing and a tenderness that threads its way through the fabric of my soul. His cock stirs awake under my palm. My gaze locks onto his, an invitation to step beyond our known boundaries and taste the nectar of love boundless and profound. "But I want more than one boyfriend," I whisper into the silence, "I've always had my heart set on three." The words feel like a confession, a secret dream now spoken into existence.

Dean's laughter, a low rumble, vibrates against my skin, and his eyes sparkle with amusement. "I don't think your sexual appetite could handle three." He teases, his guarded blue eyes reflecting a lightness that belies the weight of our conversation. But there's something else there, a challenge flickering in the depths of his gaze, an unspoken dare that rouses the restless spirit within me.

I am no virgin, having lost my innocence to the Goth guy, the only other loner at my school when I was 15. We did the deed in a cemetery in the dead of night. I know how very Morticia and Gomez Addams of us, very much so in harmony with our depressive and obsessive death state. I bled an absurd amount, which didn't deter the guy at all. Despite being satisfactory it was nothing to write home about, but it made me grasp that I like sex, a lot. I prefer casual, no strings attached, scratch the itch and never see the guy again kind of screw, says the girl that finds it hard to connect with other people, that is, until our eight-part Scooby gang came to be.

With Dean Greyson, it is different; feelings are involved; I really like him. Caving to him goes beyond a carnal dance amidst the sheets and is handing over a part of my blackened heart. For someone broken already that is like igniting a very short fuse of an unstable dynamite and not having enough time to run and hide before the devastating blow arises. But here he is, telling me I can have him and the darkest unorthodox fantasies engraved in the bowels of my soul.

I can't stay in the stagnant waters of my lost past forever; all it brought me was solitude. I followed the withered poppy petals, murky fragments of what little I can remember, here to finally escape the corroded cage I am imprisoned in. Once my past is an open book, what then? I may as well start setting the foundations of a future I long for.

"Ok, show me what you got, batman." I retort, a playfulness curling the corners of my lips as I toss his words back at him, inviting him to prove me wrong.

Without hesitation, Dean's arms that encircle me begin a downward journey, so his hands come to rest on my ass, his touch igniting a firestorm of sensation. Gravity loses its grip as I am lifted effortlessly, cradled in the strength of his embrace. This compels me to wrap my arms around his neck and my legs around his waist. I lower my face to the nook between his neck and shoulder and inhale deeply, letting his scent of leather, burning motor oil, and a hint of jasmine invade me.

Dean's strides are purposeful, each step a drumroll thundering towards an unknown crescendo as he carries me to the bed, a dark oasis amid the candlelit chamber. With a tenderness that contrasts starkly with the urgency of his movements, Dean lays me flat upon the cool sheets, the contrast between the soft bedding and the roughness of his hands sending shivers down my spine. My breath catches as his fingers work deftly, peeling away the layers of clothing that shield my skin from his searching gaze. The fabric parts, a petal unfurling, revealing the naked truth of my yearning beneath.

"Damnit, Poppy, you are going to be the death of me. You naked, it's a sight not meant for us mere mortals. I can only worship you like the dark queen you truly are." He says with a seriousness I can't rival.

"You flatterer."

Dean, carved from shadows and desire, descends upon me like a predator poised at the brink of satiation. "I am going to kiss you now."

"Is that so?" Whatever I was going to say next got

swallowed by his lips slamming into mine. His kiss starts vulnerable almost, as if the older Greyson brother is scared he's going to fuck this up. However, the second I bury my fingers in his dark brown hair and dig my nails in his skull, sucking on his bottom lip, all hell breaks loose, and the kiss turns fevered. Both our tongues wove and untangled themselves with one another's, an action that screams look at us. We might be damaged goods, but that is, in all likelihood, why we fit so flawlessly together. I hate kissing, too intimate, but this one makes me want to do it for all eternity.

Dean's mouth forsakes mine, his body creeping south. He leaves an aftermath of kisses on the way down, brushing his tongue to my exposed skin, stimulating me to a point of no return. His breath, hot and charged with primal need, fans over my wet folds, drawing a quiver that ripples through my whole being. His tongue, an instrument of fiery passion, traces the contours of my yearning with deliberate hunger. The sensation is as if a thousand whispered secrets are being etched into the fabric of my flesh, every stroke sending cascades of pleasure rippling through me.

"I knew it. You taste fucking divine, Catwoman." Dean declares, licking his lips before going back for more of my juices. This time, his tongue penetrates me, which makes me purr like a kitten. In and out, it goes before his attention moves to my bundle of nerves. I am awash in the throes of an ancient dance, each flicker of his tongue a step deeper into the labyrinth of my undulating ecstasy.

The walls of this haunted mansion, steeped in mysteries and half-remembered dreams, close around us, whispering tales of long-lost loves and forbidden desires. Dean's teeth nibble at my clit, which conjures a deluge within me, rendering me utterly and irrevocably ready. As my body convulses, the biker boy takes the window of opportunity to strip off his clothes.

He's an eye-catching specimen with his clothes on, especially when he wears his well-loved leather jacket, which is pretty much always. Without them, though, he is mouth-watering. Slender, yet with a nice muscle outline, tattoos scattered all over his fair skin, small pieces mostly until you get to his moth tattoo on the center of his chest, which seems to jump out at me

Coming back to engulfing my body with his, he tells me, "Careful, Poppy, keep looking at me like that, and I will follow you to hell," Dean thrusts into my core as he speaks that last word and pulls out after saying, "and back."

The world narrows to a single pinpoint of existence, a nexus where only Dean's relentless rhythm matters. His body, a silhouette against the candlelight, drives into mine with a ferocity that borders on the divine. Our union is a storm, a vortex of raw energy that consumes without remorse; each thrust is a testament to the insatiable force that draws us together.

Fuck, the older Greyson's cock may not be thick, but it is long, and it has a very enjoyable arch. My moans are the chorus of this dark symphony, rising above the crackle of flames and the heavy breaths that fill the air like a storm cloud ready to burst.

One of his arms, resting by his elbow and forearm, holds his weight by my head while his other hand is on my hip, gripping me with ardor. My hands have found themselves on Dean's shoulder blades, scratching at his skin until I can feel droplets of blood exude from the trauma. We move together in a dance as old as time, our bodies entwined in a desperate grasp for something beyond the reach of understanding, difficult and all-consuming. In this moment, we are not merely two souls lost in carnal bliss; we are the very embodiment of danger itself, teetering on the edge of oblivion.

"Fuck, Poppy. I don't think I can last much longer. You feel too damn good." The universe seems to tremble, contracting around us as Dean's hand slips from my hip and nestles between our fevered bodies. There is a moment, profound and shattering in its intensity when his fingers find the tender bud of my arousal and press. This pinching promise fractures my reality into splinters of pleasure.

My breath catches, held captive in the hollow of my throat, and I am suspended in the torturous space between pain and ecstasy. "Ah, Dean..." The sound spills from me, a whispered invocation, as the cresting wave within me breaks. Rapture crashes through me, a relentless tide, and I am adrift, unmoored by the force of my climax. It's a cascade of raw sensation, flooding every fiber of my being, leaving me gasping for air yet drowning in an ocean of bliss. There is only Dean and the undulating current of desire he commands with each calculated caress.

TEN

I can feel the vibrations of Dean's heart against mine, a drumbeat echoing the lingering tremors of my pulse so damn fast. The hand that he had used to unravel me slams into the mattress right next to my hip, gripping the sheets with cruelty. He thrusts in and out my core a few more times before settling himself deep in my pussy that chokes his cock with the ripples of my rapture. His length swells and jerks as his warm seed spills within me.

"Poppy." Dean groans, his arm by my head quivering with the intensity of his climax, barely holding his weight up. The heat of his body seeps into my flesh, a comforting balm to the tempestuous dance we've just shared.

We take a moment to gather our composure, calm our heavy breathing. All my past sexual rendezvous, now nothing but a bland and dull evocation when set side by side with this beautiful swarm of buzzing feelings I just consummated. They feel like Pluto, once good enough to be considered a planet, yet at the present but a faraway outsider, too small to matter.

"Wow, Catwoman, you really live up to your pet name, don't cha?" The older Greyson brother remarks, moving the hand by my hip to my raven black hair, brushing his fingers through my strands affectionately. A questioning hum leaves my throat as I arch an eyebrow. "Kitten has claws." He notes. "You made me bleed, baby."

"Oh hmm sorry."

"No. You misunderstand, I liked it. For you I would weep red, Poppy." Dean tells me.

"How about you gush something else instead?" Now he's the one raising an eyebrow in question. "Ready for round two?" I say, constricting my pussy walls around his cock.

Dean shuts his eyes, hissing at my action, his dick jumping to attention inside of me. "I stand corrected, catwoman; your sexual appetite is insatiable when awoken from its slumber." His eyes open and meet mine. "Fine." Dean utters in a hoarse broken voice as his body erects away from mine and he pulls out. This confuses me for a second, but then he commands, "On all fours, kitten. If you are going to scratch me up like a cat, I am going to fuck you like one." I seek to mask my grin by biting on my lower lip.

Immediately after planting myself in the position Dean put in a plea for, I wiggle my ass, striving to evoke without asking for his cock to go back where it belongs, inside my pussy. Instead of his dick I feel his fingers trailing up the inside of my thigh harvesting some of the juices that poured out of me, before them being pushed into my core. I purr at the delicious intrusion.

"This is to stay inside of you, Poppy. If you are just going to be wasteful with it, I ain't giving you more." Dean informs me as he starts driving his fingers in and out of me, leisurely at first and then punishingly fast.

"Greyson." I scream as he makes me blossom afresh. My arms lose their strength and my upper body slopes forward, my head coming to rest on the mattress. The older Greyson doesn't allow me a second to draw a breath and flock together any thoughts, shoving himself in my pussy and continuing with the rough pounding but with his dick instead.

I bury my face in the sheets in an attempt to keep my loud moans at bay; I love this position; guys' dicks can go farther, get balls deep in you, and with Dean's length, I am in fucking paradise.

His hands are on either side of my hips, keeping me grounded as he rams into me over and over again. I don't think I ever came down from the previous high, as my body seems stuck in this involuntary state of tremor. It's sweet agony, and I don't know if I want Dean to stop or keep going.

"Shit, Catwoman. You are not making it easier for me to last long. You keep milking me like there's no tomorrow." He comments. At least we are both suffering.

Caressing my spine up, Dean's hands journey to my throat. Once in his grasp, he pulls me to him so my back is flushed against his front while his other hand comes around my middle. The oppressive squeeze on my throat makes it so that my pleasure noises are but silent whimpers; therefore, all you can hear echoing in the room is Dean's groans, the old bed creaking, and the sensual sound of flesh meeting flesh.

That's the thing: when you are already on the edge of the precipice, it doesn't take much for you to fall, and when I hear my name being whispered like a chant, that's precisely what happens. Without ever really dying, my third orgasm drags and gives way to my forth one, a much more violent one at that. I can feel myself squirt at the force it hits me. Dean growls as he raptures along with me, gush after gush. He fills me up with his cum, his hand on my throat clenching to the crux where I can't breathe.

The older Greyson's hold on me breaks, and we collapse onto the bed, a tangle of limbs and dampened skin, our breaths emerging in ragged harmony. The candlelight flickers, casting long, quivering shadows across the room that seem almost alive, dark specters dancing to the rhythm of our heaving chests. We lay there, side by side, the boy that just gave me plentiful pleasure on his back. I lying on my front, entwined amongst the crumpled sheets, steeped in the silence that follows the storm of our union. Yet even as we bask in the afterglow, a shadow looms at the edges of my consciousness, a dark foreboding clings to the corners of the room like cobwebs.

In the dim light, the danger feels both distant and ever-present, a silent observer of the vulnerability we've laid bare. I inhale deeply, drawing in the scent of sweat and sex that permeates the air, and wonder if the ghosts of this ancient mansion have watched our passionate encounter, their spectral eyes gleaming with secrets from beyond the veil.

The flicker of the dying candlelight and the once vibrant energy that filled the room now settle into a soft lull. Having danced to the frantic tempo of desire, our hearts now slow to a gentle, synchronized rhythm. I feel the steady pulse of his heartbeat against my side, a silent testament to the life within him that so closely mirrors my own. His breath whispers promises and uncertainties in equal measure. Yet, I cannot shake the feeling that, although spent, we are anything but safe.

"It may be that my brother and I can get what we want after all." The very handsome boy with tousled dark brown hair states out of nowhere.

"What's that?" I gasp.

"You." He tells me, as his face drops to the side, so he's looking at me. Is Dean alluding to the fact that his brother does, in sooth, want me?

"But he's an asshole to me."

"Forgive his immature manners. I guess Sam thought he could never take a stab with you because of me. I did call dibs."

"Dibs? Seriously, Dean?" I ask, a bit offended by his confession.

"I might've got a bit possessive of something I did not own yet."

"I am not an object you can own, Greyson. I want boyfriends, not masters."

"No. I know. Shit." Dean rolls in bed so his front is towards me, and I do the same. "I am not proud of hmmm that, but sibling rivalry is a bitch. I did think he only wanted you because I did, however, even a blind man can see he suspires for you too. And then jealousy took over…

There's no excuse. It did pain me, the idea that the happy ever after with you for one of us would be the sadness for the other. But since you have your heart set on ending up with more than one guy…"

I interrupt Dean by saying, "What? I would give the idiot that can't get my name right a chance?"

"You know he only does that to get your attention. Ruffling your feathers is his thing with you. And don't lie to me, Catwoman, at heart, you love it." Perhaps, I do. "Just at least consider him for your little harem. Please."

"I can't believe you are asking me to get involved with your brother as I date you."

"Yeah, neither can I." He utters, sliding his arm under my head while his other drapes over my hip. "I must be delirious from all the crests we reached."

"I'll think about it," I murmur into the darkness that creeps in from the room's corners, swallowing the last vestiges of light. The words hang between us, heavy with thoughts unspoken and decisions yet to be made. Dean is silent, but his arms tighten around me, a silent plea for understanding, perhaps, or a simple need for connection in the face of the unknown.

In this mansion of shadows and half-remembered dreams, where every stone seems imbued with ancient whispers, we are but two souls adrift, seeking harbor in each other's arms. The idea of sharing my heart with more than one, of entwining my destiny with several instead of a singular path, is as daunting as it is exhilarating. Yet there is solace here, in the rise and fall of Dean's chest, a reminder that no matter how scattered my past, the present holds its form of certainty.

Slowly, we succumb to the night's embrace, the world beyond our entangled forms fading into obscurity. Sleep beckons with sweet oblivion, promising respite from the torrent of emotions that have marked our day. As consciousness wanes, I drift on the edge of slumber, the weight of Dean's presence a grounding force against the tide of my trepidation. Outside the sanctuary of our room, the phantom manor looms, a beast of stone and spire whispering secrets into the chasm of the night. Darkness wraps around us like a shroud, thick and oppressive, foretelling tales of loss and peril that linger just out of sight. Something stirs in the depths of these walls, a malevolence born of ancient rites and forgotten bloodlines.

The air grows colder, a creeping chill that slithers beneath our cocoon of warmth, an icy finger tracing the outline of my spine. Somewhere, in the bowels of the fortress, a sound rises, a low, mournful wail that speaks of centuries-old grief, echoing through hallways and seeping through the very stones that shelter us. I shiver, a flicker of intuition igniting within me, a primal warning that danger, though unseen, watches with jealous eyes. It waits, patient and calculating, for the moment when our guard falls with the veil of sleep and the boundaries between worlds grow thin.

The scent of damp earth and decay drifts in, a subtle invasion mingling with our passion's lingering traces. It reminds us that we are never truly alone even in moments of intimacy and abandon. Somewhere in the darkness, something awaits, its hunger palpable, its intentions as shadowy as the room that now shields us from its gaze.

ELEVEN

Morning sunlight filters through the half-drawn curtains, casting a warm glow on the tangled sheets where Dean and I lay nestled in reluctant slumber. My eyelids flutter open to the new day, heavy with the remnants of dreams that slip away like mist. Dean's breath is soft against my neck, a comforting rhythm in the quiet room. I slide out from under his arm, careful not to wake him, feeling the chill of the air as I leave our cocoon of warmth. My fingers brush over yesterday's clothes crumpled at the foot of the bed; there's no point in searching for something fresh when my suitcase still lies somewhere downstairs.

I peer behind me when I hear the rustling of sheets as Dean sits up, hair rumbled, looking very suckable. "What time is it?" He asks.

I reply, "I have no idea, but I'm hungry. Let's go find the kitchen." He nods. In turns, each of us takes a shower in the adjoining bathroom and gets dressed.

The wooden floorboards creak underfoot, a whispered

protest, as we walk out of the room, Dean trailing me like a shadow. "Had fun, Aster?" A raspy male voice asks from our rear.

"Holy fuck." We turn around to come face to face with, "Samuel!" He's leaning by the wall of the room where his brother and I just spent the night, foot perched on the wall, hands in his jeans' front pockets. "Creeper much?" I ask in vexation.

Sam parts from the wall and saunters our way, stopping right in front of me. He slants his upper body in my direction so his face is a mere few breaths away from mine. "I thought you had a thing for what lurks in the shadows?" My eyes lower to his lips before rising to his pale blue eyes.

"Dude, so not cool," Dean tells our stalker.

"What?" Sam stands straight and looks dead on at the older Greyson. "Oh, come on, it's not like I camped outside your room listening in through the door to you guys go at it like porn stars." Dean folds his arms over his chest, arching an eyebrow disapprovingly. "It's not my fault I bunked in the room beside yours. And your girl-friend," the younger Greyson spits that word like it tastes awful in his mouth, "being so damn loud."

"Jealousy doesn't look good on you, brother."

"Fuck you." Sam throws at his older brother.

"Hmmm, pass. My girlfriend, " Dean stresses that one term, "tired me out." We are never going down for food at the rate this conversation is going.

"So it's official, you two are together now." Damn, Sam, in sooth, sounds hurt when he utters that. "Well, it's not like every last one of us didn't know all it would take was for you to bang to end up with each other. Long time coming, you two were. No one else had a shot." See, why does he have to say shit in such a pitiful way? He makes it hard to bleed for him.

"You could if you stop being such an idiotic man-child." Yes, the guy is frustrating and annoys the hell out of me more times than not, deliberately pushing my buttons, but I guess deep down, I do like him. We either fuck, or we will kill one another. And I would hate to have his blood stain my hands, be the cause of his last breath.

Samuel seems a shade taken back by what I just admitted, "Wait, what?"

Dean chuckles, "You should tell him, Catwoman. Put him out of his misery."

"Nah, let him sulk for a bit longer. I will unequivocally feel the absence of having him dwell on his dejection after I do so." I utter, spinning around, my raven black hair slapping Sam in the face with the sudden grace of my movement.

"Am I missing something?" Sam asks about the lack of certainty embedded in every word.

Walking away from the Greyson brothers, I catch Dean's faint murmur, "You two are as bad as each other."

All three of us descend the staircase; each step lightened by the faint hope of morning chatter and the rich aroma of coffee. I can see our bags and suitcases by the front door, which means someone thoughtfully went outside to grab our things. But as we enter the kitchen, a thick silence greets us. The rest of the Scooby gang sits huddled around the table, their faces etched with somber lines that don't belong in the gentle clutches of dawn.

"What's up?" My voice cuts softly through the stillness, inviting secrets to unfold.

Henry looks up, his normally mischievous eyes now clouded with concern. "Went out to get our stuff from the car," he starts, hesitating as if the next words are heavier than the rest, "and found footprints. They lead straight to the front door."

A jolt of alarm sends a shiver down my spine, ice cold and sharp. "Show us," I demand, heart racing with a pulse of adrenaline that paints the world in sharper hues.

Outside, the sky looms overhead, vast and indifferent. Henry points to the ground just by the cars, and the footprints are pressed into the dew-soaked earth. They are large, too large to be human, with jagged edges that speak of claws or nails. Each impression is deep, deliberate, etched with a precision that suggests intelligence, a hunter stalking its prey. The tracks lead unswervingly to the house, a silent invasion that stops abruptly at the front door.

My breath catches in my throat as the reality sinks in. The footprints tell a story none of us want to read. They have an otherworldly quality, as though the creature that made them walked straight out of a nightmare and into our world. It's as if the ground whispers warnings of an evil presence that has breached our sanctuary.

"Did... did it get inside?" Dean's voice trembles slightly, mirroring the fear that tightens my chest.

No one answers, but we all know the question hangs over us, a specter more chilling than the morning air. We exchange glances, each of us silently preparing for the possibility that danger lurks closer than we ever imagined.

The imprints on the ground are a harbinger, a dark omen that casts a long shadow over the fragile peace of our gathering. As we stand there, the weight of the unknown presses down upon us, heavy as stone, and I can feel the threads of our reality fraying at the edges.

Gathering around the grotesque impressions marring the earth, we huddle closer, drawing warmth from shared unease. The rising sun does little to chase away the chill that clings to our bones. I find my gaze lingering on the footprints, trying to unravel their secrets, as whispers of dread and wonder ripple through the group.

"Could it be a creature from the old tales?" Luke asks in a hushed tone.

"Or perhaps a prank meant to unsettle us," Sam suggests, though the hope in his words feels as fragile as a cobweb.

I kneel beside the nearest print, my fingers hovering above its chilling outline, not quite daring to touch. "Neither beast nor trickster leaves a mark such as this," I murmur, my voice soft but steady. The footprints are an omen, a shadow cast upon our hearts, and I cannot, will not, let it go unanswered.

With a resolve that surprises me, I stand, brushing the dew from my hands. The others watch me, their eyes wide, reflecting the turmoil of thoughts I feel mirrored in my soul. "We'll find the origin of these tracks," I declare, more to convince myself than them. "The truth is hidden amidst the forest's whispers."

TWELVE

The urgency of my mission propels me forward, the footprints calling to me like a siren's song. With each step, the darkness cast by the dense grove of cypress trees draped in a heavy veil of Spanish moss in this never-ending bayou seems to press in, eager to swallow us whole. Branches claw at my clothes, a tangible reminder of the dangers lurking just out of sight. The air within its confinements is thick with the musk of decay and the sharp tang of fear, both foreign and intimately familiar.

"Stay close," I instruct, my voice barely above a whisper, yet it cuts through the silence like a blade. We move as one, a chain of souls bound by the desire to unearth what lies hidden.

Darkened silhouettes dance at the corner of my vision, fleeting and elusive, between the dangling vines falling from the canopies of gray bark trees like nooses ready to hang us. While the underbrush rustles with the movement of unseen critters. Every sense is heightened, every nerve taut with anticipation.

The footprints carve a dark path, a trail etched with malice and mystery. We follow, hearts thundering against ribs, knowing that what awaits us in the depths of the swamp may well be the very embodiment of our fears. Yet onward we tread, for turning back is no longer an option when the unknown beckons so insistently, promising revelations or damnation in its enigmatic embrace.

"Maybe they are gator impressions," Ben observes, seeking solace in what's tangible instead of the possibility of something unknown.

"Even though alligators extend their legs so their bellies don't drag, their long tails do. I don't see a line cutting through the footprints; therefore, I don't think that particular swampy creature did this." Oliver explains.

"Way to crush Benny's hopes for something that is still scary yet less so than what it very likely is," Luke says, gasping Ben's hand to ease his anxiety.

We arrive at a fork in our pilgrimage through this paradise infected with bloodthirsty mosquitoes, where the footprints seem to take many directions. I feel the weight of leadership as eyes turn to me, their gazes mingled with trepidation and resolve. We must trace these spectral imprints to their source, yet the thought of separation hangs heavy like the mist that clings to the manor's ancient stones. Which road do we take? Where do we want to go? I don't know. Then, it doesn't matter.

"Let's break into pairs," I suggest, my tone steady despite the fluttering in my chest. That way, we can cover more ground." The decision is met with somber nods; we all understand the dangers of our endeavor.

Rosie takes my side in a heartbeat, which means she's coming with me. "Hmmm, baby, I would feel better if you were with me," Henry tells her.

"Sorry, us girls need to stick together in this male-infected world." Rosie declares.

"What does that have to do with anything?" Henry questions his girlfriend.

"Ugh, fine. Poppy and I need some alone time, so," she comments as she weaves her arm with mine, "see you on the other side, boys." Each duo takes a different course, leaving Rosie and me to face the forest's gaping maw, where the footprints beckon us deeper into its shadowy heart.

Rosie's arm drops, and she holds my hand instead, squeezing it briefly and her touch grounding. "We've got this, Poppy." She says, and I draw strength from her unwavering spirit, from the bond we share that has weathered countless storms. Together, we follow the trail, the earth beneath our feet soft and yielding, as though it too whispers secrets of things buried and best left undiscovered.

"So, you and Dean have finally done it." Rosie betrays all of a sudden.

I chuckle, "Oh, I see why you wanted to pair off with me. You want to gossip."

"No," she drags that one word out before continuing in a sweet as-pie voice, "I want you to distract me. Henry would zero in on all the bad shit that can happen to us in this depressing and scary swamp. And complain about being hungry."

"Aww, you do love him," I utter teasingly.

"Oh, shut up, which you know I do. Now, back to you and Dean. And Sam? What happened there?"

The silence is a living thing, oppressive and thick, wrapping around us like a shroud. I can hear the ragged cadence of our breaths, too loud in the muted hush that has fallen over the bayou. Our path is a scar upon the earth, leading us deeper into shadows and whispers. A bird's haunting cry pierces the stillness, and Rosie's grip on my hand tightens. "Just a bird," I murmur, though the sound seems to mock us, a reminder that we are intruders here.

"Right." She clears her throat. "So," Rosie ain't letting it go; she's relentless. I'm just going to have to spill the deeds.

"Yeah, me and Dean had sex." She squeals in excitement, which pulsates with the gust that brushes past us. "We are boyfriend and girlfriend."

"Oh my gosh, I know that right this instant, we are chasing shadows that leave grisly footprints in the mucky and muddy ground, but I knew that haunted mansion could be the setting of fairytales."

Our steps quicken as we delve further into the swamp, each print an echo of dread that pulses through the soles of our boots. The footprints are fresher here, the edges sharp and defined, cutting through the underbrush with sinister precision.

"I told him about wanting three," the word soulmates pops into my head, and I end up yelling. "I dare say Dean's ok with it since he's trying to set me up with his brother."

"Sam!" she howls, setting birds off in a hasty departure. A sinister chill slithers down my spine, and I can't shake the feeling that we're being watched, that eyes unseen are tracking our every move.

"Can you feel it, Rosie?" My voice is tight, barely audible over the whispering leaves. "The bayou, it's alive somehow."

She nods, eyes scanning the darkness creeping on us from all sides. The ashen cypress trees loom like silent gargoyles, their twisted forms casting grotesque shadows that writhe and contort with our passing. There's a heaviness in the air, a suffocating embrace that seeks to smother the courage we cling to so desperately.

"Stay alert, ok?" I whisper, and Rosie's hand finds mine once more after letting go of the joy of our conversation, a lifeline amidst the encroaching gloom. The impressions lead on, and with each step, the certainty grows within me: we are not hunters on this trail but the hunted. And whatever hounds our steps are closing in, its presence is a dark promise woven into the very fabric of the swamp.

"Nice to hear that I wasn't wrong about Sam liking you," Rosie notes. "Poppy Elise Hartwood is dating both Greyson boys; now there's a tale for the ages."

The footprints stretch before us like breadcrumbs from a tale best forgotten, each an imprint of dread. I feel the weight of every step, the burden of fear growing heavier with the knowledge that we are far from any sanctuary.

"Me and Samuel aren't... anything yet."

"Yet, being the key word in that sentence. Oh, that reminds me, you were late for breakfast this morning, so you missed it, but I believe you weren't the only one that got dick last night."

"Rosie, you and Henry have been going out forever; you get lucky all the time," I remark.

"Not me, silly. We did make love, but that's not the point; I am talking about Luke and Benny. When Henry and I arrived at the kitchen, Ben had Luke trapped against the island, their lips on the verge of meeting. I might've awed out loud, which disenchanted the whole moment, and they pulled away from each other. But the vibes oozing out of those two unquestionably screamed freshly fucked."

I had noticed the hand grasp between them before, their eyes following an invisible thread to one another's and locking. The swift twitch of their lips as Luke and Ben fought a bashful smile summoned up by something just between them. Forget my love story; theirs would be a great read.

A sudden and sharp branch snaps behind us, and we freeze. Our eyes meet, reflecting the same question: friend or foe? But the bayou remains silent as if holding its breath, and we move forward once more, hearts pounding a frantic rhythm against our ribs.

"Ok, I think that means enough chit-chat." Even though I am thankful for our talk, it kept my mind busy and, for the most part, off of the impending peril just around every corner. "Let's just find the bloody end of this."

As the canopy above thins, a soft, unnatural glow beckons us onward, and we emerge into a clearing that should not be. Grey bark trees encircle it like sentinels, their branches interlocking to form a barrier that feels both protective and imprisoning. The footprints converge here, a tangled dance of countless feet that leads to nothing and ends at nothing. A sense of wrongness permeates the air, as tangible as the mist that clings to our skin.

Have we just found ourselves in the gorge of the bayou about to be devoured by it?

THIRTEEN

"Poppy." Rosie's voice is a thread of sound woven into the tapestry of unease that envelops us.

"Shh." I hold a finger to my lips, eyes scanning the clearing. Something moves at the edge of vision, a flicker of darkness that could be a trick of the light or not. My pulse thrums in my ears, a drumbeat of warning that resonates with the ancient trees. This place is a secret kept for centuries, a heart whose beat echoes the rhythm of fear. And we stand at its center, trespassers in a world that does not welcome us.

I see it, engraved in the ashen trees dressed in Spanish moss surrounding us, runes. "Look," I say, my voice barely above a whisper, yet it slices through the silence with the precision of a blade. "This has to be old, really old. But it's too deliberate to be mere vandalism. It's purposeful."

My fingertips trace the grooves of a symbol carved into the barks around us. This intricate design speaks of ancient rites and forgotten languages. It's as though the trees bear the weight of a story untold, their skin etched with secrets that beg to be heard. The carving appears alive, pulsating with a rhythm that chimes with my heartbeat, drawing me deeper into its enigmatic embrace. Goosebumps rise on my flesh, not from the chill in the air but from the realization that this symbol is a precursor, a piece of a puzzle we're only just beginning to assemble.

"What the hell?" I hear Samuel utter as he and his brother appear in the clearing that the footprints they were following also led them here. Slowly, the rest of the group emerges into this hub where we stand, where they all trace the cravings on the tree trunks, with looks of horror and awe on their faces.

Dean steps closer to one of the runes; his brows furrowed in concentration. "It's like a marker," he muses aloud. "A signpost or a warning. Maybe it's trying to tell us something."

"Or usher us somewhere," I add, my mind racing with possibilities. "There's the intent here. It's part of a larger design, something we're meant to find."

The eight of us huddle around the symbol, our shadows merging with the darkness of the clearing. The same insatiable need for answers binds us, a yearning that tugs at our souls with invisible threads. Yet, in the presence of this cryptic herald, excitement wars with fear, and the thrill of discovery is tainted by the taste of danger on our tongues.

"Does anyone else find it weird that all routes shepherd us to the same place? This feels like a trap." Oliver remarks.

The swamp seems to close around us, the trees whispering cautionary tales in a language only the wind understands. The symbol now feels like an omen etched in the very heart of this clearing, where every rustle of foliage, every squishy echo of something treading on the muddy ground, is a potential threat lurking just beyond sight. Our breaths come out in misty clouds that mingle with the creeping fog, painting the scene with strokes of apprehension.

"Well, it does feel like whatever made those footprints might be watching us right now." Rosie murmurs, her eyes darting to the shadowy fringes of the clearing.

"Let them watch," I say, more bravely than I feel, "we won't be intimidated by some swampy specter." But as the words leave my lips, a cold breeze stirs the veil of Spanish moss, carrying a low, guttural growl, freeing us in place. The sound is neither human nor animal, a disturbing reminder that we've stepped into a realm where the rules of the natural world no longer apply. My heart pounds against my chest, and each beat echoing the dread that coils tightly around my spine.

"Ok, I am out of here." Ben declares. "We can harp on this shit in the confines of the mansion."

This spot betrays this aura of Asphodel Meadows, the fields of ashes, in the Greek underworld, where the souls of the dead can get enslaved, bit by bit, turning into trees if they depart the living world with unfinished business or regrets. Damn, is that what's happening here? I don't want to leave. I feel like I have been running away from my past all my life, and now that I'm here, I want to say rotted, even when peril is knocking at the door. Am I so engrossed in my rue that I will get myself and my fellow companions captured and forever imprisoned in this limbo?

"Yeah, we should go," I announce.

"Hold on, perhaps we should take photos of the slashes."

"Way ahead of you," Luke tells Oliver, raising the camera in his hand. The boy with ash-brown hair grabbed it from Sam's car before we began this journey into the unknown. Smart. I am sure he has been documenting everything.

"Ok, let's go then." Sam sets forth.

We trace the footprints back towards the eerie stone manor, and somehow, our steps are more hasty and rash than before. Liliana's forewarning, a white noise, rings in our ears, compelling us to return to our only asylum in this secluded spot in Transylvania, Louisiana.

It doesn't take us long to reach the locus where the impressions merge into a singular trail, its direction unerring, leading us inexorably back to the towering edifice of stone. Our investigation has come full circle, leaving us with more questions than answers. Each step amplifies the sense that something evil watches waits, and desires to draw us into its dark embrace.

"Hey, Jasmine, can we talk?" The younger Greyson asks as he rushes to my side, which rivals my pace.

"What about?" I throw back at him, keeping my eyes peeled in the path ahead.

"What you said before, in the old but lavish shack?" His choice of words makes me chuckle.

I gaze at him then, my alien yellow eyes taking him in. From his dark brown hair, a shade darker than his older brother's, that unlike Dean's, has seen a comb, to his stunning facial features, strong jawline, narrow, sharp nose, high cheekbones, and coming to his lean physique with nice enough ridges to drool over. Samuel's pale blue eyes snap to me when I take too long to answer him, a smirk arising on his lips when he notices me ogling him up.

Just when I am about to spill my guts out about my hunger for three partners and that I might want him to be one of them alongside his brother, the air around us shifts, making me wince. "Can you feel it?" I ask, my voice barely above a whisper. "It's like the air is thick with bloody anticipation."

"Or dread," Oliver adds softly as he turns up at my other side, his eyes reflecting the shadows that dance between the trees. The footprints weave a path back to the heart of our mystery. I cannot shake the disquieting thought that we are being herded, manipulated by an intelligence that remains veiled from sight.

Or like something does not desire me to tell Samuel the perverted tastes buried deep within my blackened heart. Panic claws at my throat as the world narrows to the thudding of my heart, echoing the drumbeat of impending doom. We hurry up our pace further, the ground beneath us hard and unyielding, and the once benign bayou now a labyrinth of gnarled branches reaching out like skeletal fingers.

"Something isn't right." I gasp, the words slicing through the heavy air. "We're not alone."

A shiver cascades down my spine, and without warning, the swap erupts into a cacophony of shrieks, the sound piercing, alien, and utterly terrifying. It reverberates off the phantom manor walls, encapsulating us in a sonic web from which there seems no escape. We freeze, our breaths caught in a collective gasp, as the essence of fear incarnate wraps its icy tendrils around us.

"Run!" Dean shouts, the command laced with urgency, propelling us forward. Yet even as we sprint towards the illusory safety of the mansion, I know this is only the beginning. With each heartbeat, the chilling symphony crescendos, a harbinger of horrors yet to be unveiled.

FOURTEEN

The ancient wood of the mansion's front door groans under our collective shove. I am the last one in, and as I step through the threshold to safety, I gaze behind me. I swear I see three majestic dark silhouettes peeking through the shadows the grove of Cypress trees cast just before a hand grabs me by the elbow, pulling me deeper into our asylum, and the door closes. The echo of its thud pulsating through the cavernous entrance hall like the last beat of a dying heart. We press against it as if our bodies could meld into the grain, become part of the phantom manor's defenses against the terrors without.

My chest heaves, each breath a shard of ice in my lungs, and for a moment, I savor the relative safety of these stone walls. The air is tinged with the musty scent of forgotten memories, and shadows cling to the corners, whispering secrets I'm not sure I want to hear. Liliana's warnings, once cryptic riddles, now seem prophetic, her green eyes haunting me with their unspoken knowledge.

"Could it be?" Sam's voice cuts through my reverie, trembling like a leaf clinging to a branch in autumn's chill. "The creatures. Is that why Liliana cautioned us?"

His gaze flits from one shadow to the next, a deer caught in the snare of impending darkness. There is an earnest trepidation behind those pale blue eyes, the kind that seeps into your bones and nests there. He stands small amidst the grandeur of the entrance hall, his scholarly demeanor stripped away by raw, human dread. And though he speaks softly, his words carry the weight of all our fears, hanging between us like a shroud.

Somewhere beyond these walls are creatures born of nightmare prowl, their malevolent presence tangible darkness that seeks to swallow us whole. Are they part of my forgotten past or something written in upon the fabric of reality to shepherd me away from what I seek?

"Did y'all see anything?" Dean's hushed tone is laced with horror, his skin pale beneath the flickering light. It flickers across his face, throwing grotesque shapes onto the walls that play tricks on our already frayed nerves. The unknown dangers outside have breached the sanctuary of his mind, and I can feel the tendrils of fright creeping into my thoughts.

Liliana's veiled cautionary tales resonate with newfound clarity, a chilling prelude to the horrors that stalk us now. We stand on the precipice of terror, the mansion no longer a mere structure of stone and mortar but a bulwark against a darkness that seeks to devour us.

The words about what I might've witnessed out there choked me. One second, they are on the tip of my tongue, ready to be told, and the next, I am forced to swallow them down, a voice in my head screaming that they are for me alone, not to be shared with others. Whatever does that mean? Great, even my mind is ominous now.

Luke's laughter cuts through the stillness like a sword, each peal bouncing off the stone walls and ringing in my ears. Adrenaline courses through his veins, starkly contrasting the icy tendrils of fright that grip mine. "What a rush, huh?" He exclaims, eyes gleaming with the thrill of what we've escaped.

Rosie, ever the anchor in our storm, lets out a sigh that seems to carry the world's weight. She stands beside the boy with ash brown hair and hazel eyes, her face a canvas of worry, green eyes dimmed by the shadows that linger in our refuge. "Luke, this is serious," She chides, her voice carrying the gentle firmness that can only come from deep concern masked as frustration. Her fingers twitch at her side, fighting the urge to reach out and shake some sense into him. But she doesn't; she knows it's his way of coping, of chasing away the darkness with his indomitable spirit.

"What the hell have you brought us into, Poppy?" Ben asks. "What demons have you brought down upon us?"

"Hey, this isn't on her." The younger Greyson hisses at the boy with dirty blonde hair and old-world blue eyes. "We all choose to come, to follow Poppy in her journey to the past." Wait, did Samuel say my actual name?

Amidst the clash of light-hearted bravado, caution, and finger-pointing, Henry steps forward, his gaze sweeping over the grandeur of the entrance hall. His Nordic blue eyes are sharp and analytical, painting him as the problem solver we've all come to rely on, the one who navigates us through chaos with a joke and a plan. "Let's not test our luck with whatever's out there again." He suggests, as if it is as simple as that, his tone steady despite the undercurrent of urgency. "There's plenty within these walls to explore. Hidden passages. Forgotten rooms. Let's see what secrets this old place holds."

He's right. The haunted mansion is an enigma, a labyrinth of history and mystery that beckons us with silent whispers. It promises answers and conceals dangers, and I feel the pull of its allure, a siren call to delve deeper into its heart, away from the creatures that lurk beyond the door.

"Good idea, baby," Rosie says, her front meeting his side and her arms going around his middle in a tight hug. "Maybe we can smooth our fear by digging the buried tales within these walls. That out to distract us." Henry drapes one of his arms over her shoulders, lowering his head to kiss her forehead, a soft moan escaping her lips.

"Alright then," I murmur, my voice threading through the stillness, "we explore this dwell. There must be something here that can help us understand... everything." The others nod, their faces etched with relief and resolve, their eyes meeting mine with a quiet intensity. Bound by more than fate, we are woven together by the desire to uncover the mysteries that have trapped us since our arrival.

Oliver's sudden spark of recollection pierces the somber mood, his voice rising with buoyancy that feels almost out of place. "Liliana showed us the secret tunnel hall thingie once, remember? It could lead to, well, who knows what?" His meadow green eyes gleam with the thrill of potential discoveries, his restless spirit never quite quenched by the mundane. "Let's check it out." He says, enthusiasm bubbling in his words as if adventure runs through his veins instead of blood. And despite the uncertainty tugging at the corners of my mind, I am swept up in his excitement, a moth drawn to the promise of light in the darkness.

"I don't recall her telling us about a tunnel," Rosie notes.

"It was when you girls were resting in the drawing room," Dean tells her. "She found us wandering,"

"We got lost," Oliver interjects.

Despite the interruption, the older Greyson continues, "and mentioned it when we walked past it on our way to you."

"Ok, shall we then, gang?" I ask.

With renewed vigor, we race upstairs, our footsteps resounding against the stone, a drumbeat calling us to delve deeper into the heart of this manor. Our ascent is frantic, a flight from the creeping dread that gnaws at the edges of our courage. The stairs stretch endlessly, spiraling upwards like a coiled serpent, each step a defiant march toward the veiled truths hidden within these walls.

"Hey, does anyone else deem it strange that these candles were dead this morning, its wax melted into a puddle, and now they have flourished, standing proud once more, and lit?" Luke sets forth, and as we reach the landing, the atmosphere is urgently lit. The shadows cast by our flickering candles dance across the stone, teasing us with glimpses of what lies beyond. The air is thick with the scent of age and disuse, a pungent reminder of the secrets that have slumbered undisturbed for centuries.

"That is odd," is Sam's answer.

"Perhaps Miss Ravenshadow came over and set out to lighten up the place and chase away the darkness for us," Rosie comments, her voice letting slip that she doesn't believe in the gospel she spreads. Lilliana told us she wouldn't be back until the end of our stay.

"Or maybe the ghosts did it." We all turn to Luke at his outlandish words delivered with such seriousness that we almost give credence to them. "This place is fucking haunted. Oh, or it could be that this mansion is enchanted, and shit just magically happens."

Bewilderment takes shape in all of our faces. "Dude." Henry pleads. "I am sure there's a way more logical explanation than any."

"I think sage and sober went out the window the moment those unnatural footprints tore through the web that makes up our concept of the real world and how things are."

"Here!" Oliver exclaims, pulling us from Luke's reasoning and spurring us back to the mission at hand. The boy with tousled medium-length light brown hair, meadow green eyes, and a face smeared with freckles all along his cheeks and nose stands by the wall where the faint outline of a door emerges from the darkness. "This is it."

FIFTEEN

My fingers are poised a hair's breadth from the cold stone, feeling the vestiges of ancient magic thrumming beneath the surface. With each motion I trace in the air, patterns learned from... wait, where have I acquired the knowledge about this rite? I feel a part of my fragmented past stitching together, a tapestry woven from shadows and whispers. The hand pattern is complex, a dance of fingers that speaks to a time when such gestures could command the very essence of the world. My motions are deliberate and precise, each unlocking memories buried deep within the haunted manor's heart and, perhaps, within my own.

As the last gesture falls into place, a faint click resonates through the silence. A shiver travels up my spine, not from the chill of the stone but from the realization that we stand on the precipice of discovery, and I made it so that it could transpire.

The door, as old as the secrets it guards, creaks open with a sound like a mournful sigh, surrendering to the persistence of the present. Before us, a cobweb-infested tunnel yawns wide, its maw leading downward into an abyss where light fears to tread. The steps carved from stone vanish into pure blackness, inviting us, tempting us to shed the comfort of the known for the allure of the hidden and the forbidden.

"Is anyone going to ask the question we are all thinking?" Samuel queries the group. "No? Wolfsbane, what the hell? Where did that," the younger Greyson seeks to mimic my finger movement through the air, "come from?" I see we are back to him calling me by other flower names, the time before, in all likelihood, a fluke on his part. A raise of my shoulders is my answer since I don't have the faintest idea.

"Ha, see magic?" Luke unceremoniously observes.

"Who cares how it came about? The thing is open; let's go in." The older Greyson remarks as he winds up right next to me, his hand settling on my lower back, his touch telling me that he will be there for me no matter how weird shit gets. I turn my head, tilting it back to gaze up at him. When his piercing blue eyes meet my yellow ones, I smile his way. "I got you, Catwoman." He mouths.

I revolve for us to be facing one another, thrusting out one of my hands to the nape of Dean's neck and tugging his head down as I stand on my tippy toes, bullying us into a kiss in front of the whole Scooby gang. It's chaste but still provokes awes, and grunts from a certain someone and… Oliver? The moment our lips part, my eyes fall upon the boy with meadow green eyes, which happen to be downcast, his aura wailing hurt, screaming envy, and whispering desire.

"Come on, Wolfsbane," Samuel taunts, "escort us into the belly of this beast already."

Glances are exchanged, silent questions mirrored in each other's eyes, Sam's wide with a childlike fascination tinged by trepidation, Luke's alight with the undimmed spark of adventure, and Rosie's clouded by a concern that draws her brows together like storm clouds ready to burst. The air around us feels charged, as if the mansion holds its breath, waiting for our next move. Our footsteps resonate, a hushed symphony against the cold, unyielding stone beneath our feet, as we stand on the threshold of the unknown.

With a steadying exhale, I step forward, ready to shepherd my friends down. "Fuck its dark. Pass me one of those candelabras." I get handed a three arms candle holder, a beautiful antique corroded brass piece with hues of blues and greens tarnishing its, usually dusky shade of yellow, surface. I feel like Belle holding Lumière in her tour of the Beast's castle. "Right, here we go."

It is as though the tunnel recognizes me, the heavy silence wrapping around my shoulders like the cradle of a long-lost friend. The darkness is not just a lack of light; it is a tangible entity, filled with the whispers of my fragmented childhood, urging me to piece together the memories that flit through my mind like moths to a flame. Each step I take is laden with the weight of years spent dreaming of this place, the manor that haunted me with its ghostly siren call, now answered.

The tunnel strangles' us, a serpent carved from the earth's underbelly, its skin adorned with the ancient silk of cobwebs. They cling to my fingers, sticky tendrils that seem to pulse with a life of their own, as if the very mansion seeks to ensnare us in its secrets. My breaths come in ragged gasps, the damp air filling my lungs with the musty scent of decay and the iron tang of long-dried blood.

Shadows dance at the edges of my vision, skittering away when I try to focus on them, playing tricks on my mind in the pitch-black. We are interlopers here, trespassers in a domain of darkness that has slumbered untouched by the sun's rays for millennia.

The chill seeps through the soles of my shoes all the way to my bones, a creeping cold that heralds the descent into the earth's embrace. I watch my breath form ghostly wisps in the air, mingling with the trembling light of our slowly dying three candles as they cast an otherworldly glow upon the walls. Here, in the bowels of the manor, time seems to stand still, each droplet of condensation on the stone like a silent witness to the centuries that have passed.

Our little gang, an unlikely assembly of souls bound by fate's fickle hand, draws closer together, as if proximity could ward off the discomfort that clings to us as palpable as the cobwebs we brush aside. Dean's steady presence just behind me is both reassuring and disquieting, for I feel the weight of expectation resting upon my shoulders; the unspoken trust that I will lead us not only into the shadowed depths but also out again.

The tunnel narrows, forcing us into a single file, a line of anxious pilgrims journeying towards an altar of uncertainty. My pulse thrums in my ears, a staccato counterpoint to the soft sounds of our passage, leather on stone, the occasional scraping of metal, the calm cadence of our breathing. This underground world holds its secrets close, shrouded in the musty veil of antiquity. Though I cannot name the source of my trepidation, it coils tighter around my core with each downward step.

Suddenly, the mood shifts, the atmosphere charged with an electric sense of urgency. The tunnel turns abruptly, and there, just beyond the reach of my light, a deeper blackness beckons, a void that promises as much terror as it does revelation. It is a pit, a maw, an abyss into which we are irresistibly drawn, and the deeper down we go the certainty of danger mounts.

"How much further down does this thing go?" Rosie asks, her voice shaky from either the cold or fear, still she presses onward, we all do, driven by a primal need to confront the enigma that has called us here.

The stale air teems with the echoes of those who may have walked these paths before us, their fates etched into the very stones that now guide our way down.

"Father Ossian shared a story once that got passed down to him by a pastor friend of his from Newchurch, England, about a copper and a guy from… New Zealand, I believe it was, and how they messed with a house it was said the Devil lived upon, to never be seen again." Ben narrates out of the blue. Shadows writhe against the walls, as though responding to his haunting tale, morphing into grotesque shapes that blink, threatening to burst forth into malevolent life.

"Ben, what the fuck?" Henry howls at the boy with dirty blonde hair. "What does that have to do with anything?"

"Just that they went down into the bowels of a house too, and that's where they meet the Devil and their fate."

"Sounds like a cock and bull story if you ask me, Benny boy. A devilish yarn spun by your church to scare you into being part of the herd, turn you into the perfect submissive faithful it so desires." Luke tells Ben.

"And besides it has not been implied that the Devil lives here," Dean adds, "whence, I am sure, we are fine."

"No, but perhaps his servants do." I speak in a hushed tone, my words getting swallowed by the gloom that grows palpable, a living thing whose whispers, of forgotten tales and lost legacies, are louder than my own. I am getting worried about Ben, if the demons that lurk just out of sight in this place don't get him, I think the ones that plague his mind, forced in there by his God-fearing parents, will.

The absence of light itself has been, bit by bit, eating up at the edges of ours, while wrapping its tendrils around us, attempting to snuff out the fragile flame of our determination as well. Yet we carry on, drawn by an insatiable curiosity, a collective yearning for the elusive truths that have danced just beyond our grasp. It feels as if we are chasing ghosts through the bowels of time, phantoms of a past that refuses to surrender its secrets without a fight.

The walls seem to breathe with the weight of centuries. I can't shake the feeling that they're watching us, sentient guardians of the bloody history they encase. Our steps echo in a lullaby of melancholy, the sound bouncing off the stones and back to us, a reminder of our solitude in this subterranean expanse. In the oppressive silence between our footfalls, I hear the whispers of my thoughts, reflecting on the enigma of our quest, the sad understanding that what lies ahead may hold answers we are not prepared to receive.

Abruptly, the constricting passage yields to a grander void, and the tunnel widens into a cavernous space that drinks in our candlelight greedily. Darkened silhouettes play across the threshold, revealing fleeting glimpses of relics that are as much a part of the manor as the stones themselves. The air is thick with the musk of decay and the heavy scent of earth, hinting at the chamber's long repose from the touch of living hands.

"Holy moly, guys, are you seeing this?" Henry asks in awe. We pause at the precipice of discovery, our breaths catching in our throats as we take in the sight before us. There is a palpable sense of crossing an invisible boundary, stepping through a veil that separates the known from the forbidden.

A shiver courses through me, not from the chill that clings to the ancient artifacts but from the realization of how far we've come, and how deep we've ventured into the heart of darkness.

As we stand at the entrance of the underground chamber, ready to pierce the shadows that guard its secrets, I feel the weight of the unknown pressing down upon us. It is urgent, intense; a silent scream that beckons us forward into the abyss. The mood is thick with foreboding, an ominous prelude to the dangers that surely lurk within the hidden recesses of this forgotten sanctum.

The sensation of being watched intensifies, the air charged with a presence that is felt rather than seen. I can almost taste the tang of metal and dust on my tongue, the remnants of a time when these halls thrummed with life now lost to the ages. We steel ourselves against the fear, against the dark whispers that urge us to turn back, even as we step over the threshold, driven by a desperate need to confront the peril that awaits.

The chamber holds its breath, and so do we, teetering on the edge of revelation and ruin.

SIXTEEN

My footsteps echo on the stone floor, reverberating through the vast expanse filled with the silent witnesses of centuries past. Hundreds of artifacts line the walls, their shadows doing a macabre and grotesque dance in the flickering candlelight I hold aloft. It's going to be hard to explore the extent of this chamber with only this lustre in my hand.

All of the sudden the whole cavernous room is bathed in light, like someone just hit a switch. "What," my breath comes out in a mist, mingling with the dust that has settled over old books and tapestries which drape the walls with their faded glory.

"Mirrors." Oliver remarks, pointing all over the chamber at the reflecting surfaces gleaming thanks to the burning candles in the candelabra I have a dead grip upon. "It's like the tombs in the Valley of the Kings in Egypt, where they were able to bring sunlight into the deepest part of it by simply planting the looking glass in the right positions throughout the long corridors. Isn't it astounding?"

"Indeed." I say back to the boy with messy medium length light brown hair.

Behind me there seems to be a nicely placed hook where I can perch my candelabra and keep the room alight. Once I set it down, my gaze wanders over the threads of history woven into the fabric of the tapestries all over the walls, scenes of battles, bold and vicious, frozen in time. Amongst them are darker depictions that border on sacrilege. Figures with pallid skin and eyes like abysses, sinking fangs into the tender throats of humans. The crimson that flows seems almost to pulse within the aged fibers, whispering of a hunger that refuses to be forgotten.

"Why are there hangings flaunting images of vampires buried this far down underground?" The older Greyson asks. It's definitely odd that someone would go to all of this trouble to hole these up here. It's an unsettling reverence that clings to these images, an adoration of creatures that exist in the space between legend and nightmare.

Each step I take is heavier than the last, burdened by the weight of countless eyes that seem to follow me from the walls, and the unshakable feeling that this place holds more secrets than the stars hold light. My heart hammers in my chest, an urgent drumbeat warning me of unseen dangers lurking in the oppressive darkness of this underground archive. The musty scent of ancient leather and parchment fills my nostrils, mingling with the iron tang of imagined blood. Shadows claw at the edges of my vision, their forms undulating and twisting as though alive.

"Whoever gathered these," Rosie's voice is a calm thread weaving through the still air, "they saw beauty where others would see fear."

Her fingers brush against a tapestry, one where the stark white of vampiric fangs punctuates the velvet of night. I watch her expression shift, mingling with disgust and morbid fascination, and I feel it mirrored in my heart. It's as though we've stumbled into a temple, a shrine to creatures of myth and nightmare.

A particular one arrests my attention, a macabre ballet of death where vampires emerge triumphant, glorified in their carnage. Their faces are serene, horrifically beautiful as they indulge in their crimson feast. It's a stark reminder that things in this world are far removed from the warmth of sunlight, entities that thrive in the embrace of a never-ending night.

"Now that one is disturbing." Samuel whispers in my ear, as his front meets my back, his body warmth a pleasant shroud in the numbing bitter cold of being this below the ground.

This tight knot forms in my belly, making my core wet, which forces me to bite my lower lip to gulp down the moan that wants to sneak away. I hope this desire rise is caused by his closeness and not the bloody scene before me. I can't be that maladjusted that I am drawn to bloodsuckers, right?

"Devil's-bit, you ok?" Sam asks, one of his hands coming to rest on my belly. I jump away at the contact, perturbed by the chaos of feelings surging within me. The younger Greyson grimaces at my abrupt cut and run. "Wow, does my touch repulse you that much?" He questions in a strained yet low voice, ensuring the others don't hear him.

"What? No. Sam," shit, good going Poppy Elise Hartwood, "it's the opposite." I respond in the same calm tone.

"Oh," Samuel utters, a little taken aback by my disclosure, "ok."

"Poppy, come and look at these." Rosie calls, putting an end to mine and Sam's moment.

Before strolling to where I was summoned, I spare a last glance at the taller Greyson brother. The candlelight, cast back by the mirrors, shimmers across the spines of timeworn tomes, their titles etched in gold that no longer shines.

"Something tells me they ain't fairytale books." Rosie comments.

My fingers trace the embossed letters, a silent prayer that knowledge might arm me against the encroaching dread that coils in my stomach. "No. Probably not." I say to her. Each book feels like a puzzle piece, a fragment of a history steeped in blood and shrouded in enigma. I would happily spend eternity here, thumb through all of these pages, devouring every word written down on them and soaking up all the knowledge they offer. But time waits for no mortal, and I sense that ours is running out.

We find ourselves immersed in a sanctum that whispers of ancient reverence and dark adoration. There's so much down here, like Aladdin's cave of wonders. There are artifacts all over the place, each meticulously placed upon carved pedestals, and they seem to breathe with a life force stolen from shadowed corners of time.

My hand hovers over a chalice, its surface etched with scenes of nocturnal rituals, the silver dulled by the weight of centuries. A dark brown, almost black, stain sits at the bottom of the cup. Is that dried blood?

"Demons," Ben stands apart, his old word blue eyes locked on a fresco depicting an assembly of vampires, their faces lifted in rapture to a moon that bleeds red, "worshiped, not feared." He muses. "Reverence for the eternal, for those who have transcended death."

"People bow down to what they believe in." Luke expresses, as he goes to stand by the boy with dirty blonde hair. "For some that's God, for others the Devil, for whoever all of this belonged to it was these old folkloric beasts, it seems." One of Luke's hands seizes one of Ben's, their fingers lacing together.

"We are in Louisiana; these blood fiends have been embedded in the fabric of its history since colonial times." Oliver tells us. "It all started in 1728, when a new group of women arrived in New Orleans. As they disembarked from the ship the city folks took heed of how pale these young women were. Their luggage was also striking, a trunk resembling a casket, big enough to fit a body within. Hence the name *filles à la casquette*, or Casket Girls. Shortly after their arrival the city started to experience mysterious deaths and it's at this point that the legend branches somewhat, either they smuggled demons of blood to the New World in those chests, or the Casket Girls themselves were the vampires, using those chests to sleep in during the daylight hours."

The chill from the stone floor crawls up my spine, and I struggle to shake off the feeling of being watched by unseen patrons of this unholy gallery. We are intruders here, trespassing in a sanctuary dedicated to the immortal and the damned.

"And that everybody was Oliver's bedtime story. Goodnight." Henry jokes.

"All I was trying to say is that having credence in night fiends isn't a peculiar delusion in these parts." A puff of air slashes through the flame of our candles, compelling the lustre, and its reflection, to dance across Oliver's face, casting long, sinister shadows that coil around him like serpents.

He reaches for an ancient tome bound, its leather cracked and worn by the passage of countless years. The weight of the history within this cavernous room settles upon me like a shroud. This melancholic pall muffles even the softest sound of our breaths. I watch as his fingers trace the embossed symbols on the cover. Symbols that seem to pulsate with an energy that defies the passage of time.

I sense this pull to him, and with each step deeper into the heart of the chamber the urgency builds within me, a crescendo of primal alarm that drowns out reason. "Careful." I hear myself say, but the word is strangled, choked out by the growing intensity of the moment.

The darkness seems alive, pulsating with the whispered promises of power, of blood-soaked eternity. The air grows thick, heavy with the scent of mildew. I can taste the iron-rich essence on my tongue, a metallic tang that lingers at the back of my throat. My heart races, pounding a staccato rhythm against my ribs, as if trying to ward off the encroaching menace that slithers through the shadows. Echoes of battles long past ring in my ears, blending with our breaths, ragged and sharp with trepidation.

"Look at this, Poppy." Oliver murmurs, his voice thick with the gravity of our discovery, once I stop right next to him. His meadow green eyes reflecting the somber depths of the knowledge we unearth. He flips through the yellowed pages reverently, stopping on a passage that snags our collective attention with invisible barbs. "It says they are waiting for the queen to come back."

SEVENTEEN

An echo of sadness resonates within me, a silent lament for a queen lost to the annals of time. Yet, the sorrow is not mine alone, it seeps from the walls around us, from the artifacts that breathe with the weight of centuries. "The lost daughter of Queen Roseverden and King Alexander." My throat tightens around their names, the syllables heavy with a significance that I cannot fully grasp.

"Hey, that's the pretty girl in the painting upstairs?" The younger Greyson observes, pointing to the woman in the illustration, Queen Roseverden, a bitter feeling gouging at my heart at using the word 'pretty'. He's not wrong; she resembles the woman in the raven feathered gown, painted amid a turbulent sea and sky.

"The one with the same amber flames as Poppy, you're right." Oliver notes. "Oh, it says here that the king and queen were slaughtered by wolves, shifters." He continues, his gaze lifting to meet mine, a question unasked but understood between us. His tone is respectful, a sensitivity

121

that transcends the mere words on the page. How deep does the river of time flow, and what currents have led us to this moment?

"Loup-garous?" You can hear the unspoken prayer, in the way Rosie utters that one word, for this to be but a dark narrative embellished with fantastical beasts pulled out from the bowels of hell and nightmares. Her dark green eyes tell a tale of their own, of rupture of a reality where the only boogeymen you should fear are sick evil humans.

"Where one demon dwells, another is sure to lurk." Dean comments.

"Great, so we have vampires, werewolves. According to Luke the mansion upstairs is either infested with ghosts or enchanted by witches." Henry puts forth. "What's next, zombies?"

"Well, zombies are, in sooth, myths from the voodoo religion. If the human being is being brought back from the dead by forbidden arts or dark magic, instead of by a parasite or some sort of strange chemical is not of the possibility for this story."

"Dude, no, bad boy. We already had a storytelling moment from you." Henry reprimands the boy with a constellation of freckles in his cheeks and nose.

"You started it." Oliver says, a bit indignantly, to Henry. And this is why we work. We might be at the heart of a horror tale, a long way in the belly of the earth, going through a hoard of stuff about things that shouldn't be. However, we still keep each other from sinking and drowning in the dark treacherous waters of our dread.

Hundreds of artifacts beckon, their silent whispers tantalizingly out of reach. But it's not just the sight of old books and tapestries depicting battles and vampiric lore that ensnares me; it's the pull of something deeper, something intimately familiar.

"Poppy," a voice echoes in the recesses of my mind, distant yet achingly close. The memory surges forth without warning, a woman's hand clasping mine, her tender and urgent grip as she leads me through the woods. Her words are a mantra that haunts my every step, "You need to keep walking, Poppy, straight into town. If mummy gets taken, just run and find someone to help." The fear in her voice is palpable, a living thing that wraps around my heart and squeezes. Even now, years later, the echo of her desperation stirs the embers of panic within me, and I'm left grappling with the specter of a past that refuses to be forgotten.

"Poppy." Oliver hunts for my attention, his voice barely above a calm breath. Banishing the ghost of the memory, I turn my attention back to the present, to the task at hand. He points to an illustration of a regal figure, her face obscured by time. Could she be the lost daughter of Queen Roseverden and King Alexander? The question lingers, unspoken, between us. I ponder, if that is her, whether this lost princess looked like that when she went missing, or if this is an augury of who she would grow up.

"Why are they waiting for her return?" I muse aloud, the weight of the possibility anchoring itself to my soul. The thought is both thrilling and terrifying, for what role do I play in this unfolding drama? Am I merely an observer, or am I, too, waiting to be claimed by the shadows of my forgotten lineage?

"Wait, who's 'they' again?" Samuel asks. In the bat of

an eye, as though conjured up from the depths of my broken mind, three looming figures manifest like cobwebs in my field of vision.

"The vampires. Come on, Sam, keep up." Dean tells his younger brother.

"Could it be that these blood fiends are not just myths?" Oliver's question slices through the quiet like a blade, his meadow green eyes flickering with the hunger for truth. Each page we turn, each scroll we unfurl, brings us closer to understanding the manor's history, and our predicament. There are symbols and sigils that hint at ancient rituals, powers that once flowed through these halls, and perhaps still do.

"Guardians," I suggest out of the blue, running my fingers over the spines of countless texts on the wall beside me, feeling the impressions of time-worn lettering, "of something more profound. Something worth hiding away in this tomb of knowledge." A shiver dances down my spine as I imagine the hands that last touched these relics, were they human, or something else entirely?

"Guardians or conquerors?" The older Greyson inter-jects, his gaze lingering on a tapestry where immortal beings are exalted, worshiped by multitudes of prone figures.

"Maybe both." Luke says, as the light illuminating the cavernous room casts an eerie glow on his face. "If they have been waiting for their queen, her return could change everything."

"Change, or destroy." My voice emerges softer than I intend, a whisper of fear threading through the words. It is then that I decide it is time to retreat from this chamber of echoes, from the oppressive weight of history that threatens to swallow us whole. "Let's head back." I announce, but Oliver lingers, his hand closing around a tome bound in shadows and whispers.

"I want to read this properly in a better light." He declares, his resolve etched in the set of his jaw. He carefully closes the book, cradling it against his chest as if sheltering a fragile flame from the relentless winds of destiny.

An urgency coils within me, a serpent awakened from its slumber, ready to strike. The scent of old parchment and dust grows sharp in my nostrils, a pungent reminder of the danger lurking within these truths. We have run out of time.

"Poppy," Luke calls out, his voice a low growl in the oppressive silence, the urgency in his tone pulls me from my reverie. Luke, ever the protector, senses the peril before it manifests. His hazel eyes scan the cavern, alight with the primal instinct of a guardian facing the unknown. The shadows cling to him, envious of his vitality, of the pulse that races beneath his skin. "Something's wrong." He says, his muscular frame tense, coiled like a spring. A foreboding chill creeps up my spine as my eyes adjust to the grim realization that the darkness here is more than the absence of light, it is alive, hungry. "We need to move. Now."

"Well, we can't leave empty-handed, so just take what you want, Oliver." I command, my voice steady despite the tremor of fear that threatens to undo me. He scoops up the candelabra from its resting place. The weeping candles have created this riveting frozen waterfall of dripping wax all over the brass finish, which means that they are now too small to guide us up.

We gather, and prepare to retrace our steps through the tunnel's narrow passage, a bloody winding path that coils around us, squeezing the breath from our lungs. Oliver leads the way, his silhouette contrasting to the ink-black void that envelops us. Rosie follows, her breaths coming in short, ragged gasps, while Dean's hand finds mine in the dark, a lifeline tethering me to reality.

"Can you feel it?" The older Greyson asks, his words barely audible above the drumming of our hearts. "It's like the shadows are watching, waiting." The darkness here is alive, a pulsating entity that feeds on our trepidation.

I nod, unable to speak, my throat constricted with an ancient terror that knows my name. We are not alone in this realm devoid of sun; I can sense eyes upon us, eyes that have witnessed the turn of centuries, eyes that have seen empires rise and fall. "Keep moving." I urge, my voice a strained hiss as we hasten our pace. With every step, the questions multiply, breeding in the recesses of my mind: What lurks within the manor's heart? Who am I in this woven tapestry of fable and flesh? And what awaits us in the light beyond this cryptic gloom?

The chill of the evening air embraces us as we clamber out of the tunnel's mouth, a stark contrast to the oppressive closeness that lingered within. My hand brushes against the rough stone of the corridor we exit into. It's dark in the hall, like night has fallen since we entered the tunnel.

"Could we have been down there that long?" Rosie murmurs, her voice laced with disbelief as she peers out the window at the sky, where stars now claim their dominion.

I glance outward too, noting how the constellations seem foreign, rearranged by the unseen hands of time while we wandered in the darkness below. A sinking feeling takes root in my chest, the tendrils of twilight intertwining with an unsettling sense of displacement. How many hours had slipped through our fingers like grains of sand, unnoticed and irretrievable?

"Time must move differently here." Sam suggests, his tone even but his furrowed brow betraying his inner turmoil. "Or maybe we just lost track," He trails off.

EIGHTEEN

As I sit at the worn oak table, the kitchen is aglow with the soft light of the fireplace. I am beginning to have faith in Luke's theory that this place is enchanted because the moment we walked in this room it was already lit. Who the hell did it?

A sense of camaraderie warms the room, starkly contrasting the stone-cold walls that have borne witness to centuries of whispered secrets. Liliana's premade meals, an array of vibrant vegetables and spiced meats, are spread out before us like a mosaic of comfort. The rich aromas intertwine with the laughter of my companions create a tapestry of momentary peace in this ancient place.

We are good at this, pretending like nothing is amiss. Between the monstrous footprints that lead to a strange clearing in the swamp and being chased by shadows in the bayou, to going down to the bowels of the earth and discovering that not only vampires have ripped their way into the fabric of this reality but that it's fellow supernatural creatures, out of a fantasy read, did too. And then there's the tale of the lost daughter of Queen Roseverden and King Alexander. My mind has been stuck on the queen's eyes, which seem like the same unusual yellow hue as mine. I almost dare not say, but could we be related?

"You haven't touched your food, Marigold." Samuel points out from his seat at the table. My eyes lift from my plate to connect with the pale blue pools of the younger Greyson. "Let me rephrase that, you haven't eaten any of the food you have been shifting about in your plate."

"You should eat something." Dean tells me. "You haven't eaten anything since," he pauses in his words as a frown paints the sharp lines of his handsome face, "last night." Damn, has it been that long since I last had a bite of anything? I was starving this morning after the preceding evening's carnal mischief with the older Greyson brother. Still, at the minute hunger eludes me, my mind plagued by all the eldritch happenings that have become the forefront of this narrative. Despite that, I force a big mouth full from the mess I created in my plate just to shut the brothers up. Each bite, a reminder of the deceptive tranquility that cloaks this phantom manor.

As I chew on the stuff in my mouth, savoring the flavors Liliana has so thoughtfully prepared, my eyes relocate to Oliver. He pours over the timeworn pages of the book he retrieved from the depths of the tunnel, his brow furrowed in concentration. His ever-present empathy seems to extend towards the inanimate object, as if he could coax its mysteries out with nothing but kindness. I watch him, the way his fingers trace the faded ink, and this crave roots itself within me. I am drawn to the boy with messy, medium-length light brown hair, meadow green eyes, and a swarm of freckles that grace his fair skin. I don't think friendship between Oliver and I is enough for me anymore.

"Poppy," Oliver murmurs, not looking up from the text, "listen to this..." but his words trail off, lost in the sudden awareness of something awry, an elusive sound that tugs at the edges of our respite.

Tap... tap... tap...

At first, it's barely there, a whisper against the mansion's thick walls, as if the stones themselves speak in hushed tones. But the tapping grows more insistent, deliberate, gnawing at the fringes of our consciousness. It lures our attention away from the remnants of dinner and into the shadowy embrace of the hallway beyond.

The air in the kitchen shifts, heavy with an urgency that clings to my skin like a damp cloak. Tap... tap... tap... The knocking becomes a heartbeat, pulsating through the room, commanding us to heed its call. My heart quickly responds, mirroring the rhythm that now invades our sanctuary.

I remain frozen in my seat, the icy grip of fear seizing my limbs as I exchange looks with everyone at the table, a silent conversation fraught with alarm. We're voiceless sentinels, bound by an unspoken pact of trepidation, our eyes darting between one another's and the door. When my gaze meets Oliver's, his eyes are wide with a dawning realization of peril, his knuckles white where they clutch the table's edge. Across from us, Ben's fork clatters against his plate, the sound jarring against the steady banging on the front door. The knocking no longer hides beneath the veil of imagination, it is real, it is present, and it brings with it an omen of darkness. What stands on the other side of the door? What seeks entry?

The old tome lays forgotten as we all rise from our seats, drawn to the sound that violates the silence of the night. Each tap is a drumbeat in a symphony of dread, the prelude to an unwelcome revelation that claws at the very fabric of our safety. What once was solace now teeters on the precipice of fear, every knock an echo in the void, a harbinger of the unknown dangers that lurk just outside.

"Should we...?" My voice trails off into the gloom, the words catching like thorns in my throat. Rosie's lips part, her breath hitching as though she's about to speak, but no sound escapes. The banging grows bolder, more insistent, as if it knows we're teetering on the precipice of action.

I swallow hard, trying to dislodge the lump of fear lodged there. It was just yesterday when Liliana's words wound around us like a shroud, her green eyes piercing as she cautioned us. "Do not open the door to anyone." The memory of her warning wraps around my core, squeezing tight until I can feel each beat thrumming against my chest, a morbid echo of the knocking that refuses to fucking cease. Her cryptic counsel, once an enigma, now unfurls its meaning like the dark petals of a night-blooming flower. And with each bang on the door, the sense of foreboding that the lady of the house so effort-lessly weaved into the webs of our minds grows denser, heavier, until the air tastes of iron and dread.

Sweat beads at my temple, trickling down like the whisper of a ghost's touch, chilling me to the bone. The taping, relentless and demanding, becomes all I can hear, pounding against my skull with the force of a hammer. All else fades into obscurity; even the lingering taste of the meal our dear hostess prepared for us turns to ash in my mouth.

"Remember what Liliana said," I manage to choke out, the words brittle shards falling from my lips, "we mustn't open the door. Not now. Not at night."

"What if that's her?" Ben asks, terror exuding from every spoken word.

"Why wouldn't Miss Ravenshadow use her key to get in, you idiot?" Rosie lashes out. "And why would she caution us about something, to then," she yelps as a fresh set of thumps against the front door interrupts her. Rosie gulps down her distress before finishing her observation, "To then do that."

"Perhaps it's a test, baby, to see if we heeded to her forewarnings." Henry puts forward

But it seems that the knocking will not be ignored. It drills into us, a harbinger of nightmares clawing at the edges of reality. Something wicked waits beyond that age-worn wood, something that Liliana knew might come. Her warnings, once cryptic, now loom over us, their truth as undeniable as the terror that binds us together in this moment of shared vulnerability.

Every fiber of my being screams to flee, to hide, to do anything but face the source of our collective nightmare. Yet here we stand, paralyzed by the unknown, the darkness that claws at the door of our sanctuary, threatening to tear apart the fragile illusion of safety that Liliana's presence had once provided. Our haunted mansion has become a cage, and the beast outside is rattling its bars.

The rhythmic pounding grows louder, resonating through the bones of the manor like a pulse quickening with fright. With each knock, my heart lurches, as if trying to escape the certainty of what lies beyond our reach. I can feel the air thicken, a tangible dread settling on us like a shroud. We are but mortal souls caught in an immortal snare, there are things in this world that we will never fully understand, however now that our eyes are open to what may stalk us in the darkness, thanks to what got betrayed to us in that nether chamber, every nerve in my body is alight with the electric hum of impending doom.

Bodies drawn closer to me, the warmth radiating from them mellowing the forbidding chill that has a dead grip of me. Oliver is to my right, his hand seizing mine, our fingers lacing together. The older Greyson, comes up behind me, one of his arms going around my middle, and pulling so that my back is lined up with his front, as his younger brother gravitates right against my left side, his arm grazing mine. How odd, that this feels right, yet wrong at the same time? This is what I long for, three lovers, and these are the boys I lust after, but something seems off, amiss even. It could be down to the harrowing and dire circumstances we find ourselves upon. Yeah, I am sure that's it.

"Can you hear it?" Sam whispers, his raspy voice barely carrying over the incessant drumming at the door. "It's like... like it knows we're here, listening."

"Of course it knows." I breathe, the truth of my words

hollowing out the space inside me. Liliana's enigmatic eyes flash in my memory, a silent warning from a woman who dances with secrets. She cautioned us, her voice a melody of concealed fears, yet here we stand, transfixed by a summons that was never meant for living ears.

"Maybe it'll go away if we just ignore it." Dean suggests, but even he doesn't believe the lie his lips craft. The banging isn't merely a sound now; it's a presence, a force that seeks entrance into our haven and souls.

And then, there's Henry, brave, reckless Henry, with his sandy hair and laughter-lined eyes. I watch as something shifts within him, the protective facade giving way to the innate curiosity that has always been his blessing and curse. He walks with purpose to the front door as the rest of us hold our breaths. The question, "What the fuck is he doing," just on the tip of all of our tongues, but the words never vacate anyone's lips.

Once at the ill-omened gate, the flimsy boundary that separates us from whatever skulks out there, his Nordic blue eyes meet my amber ones, a flicker of unspoken challenge there, but also an earnest desire to shield us from whatever malevolence taunts us from the shadows.

"Guys, I..." the boy with sandy blonde hair starts, and I am already shaking my head in a disapproving manner. Still, his hand has by now reached the brass handle of the door, his voice trailing off into uncertainty.

Rosie moves as if to stop her boyfriend, her plea a desperate whisper carried on the wings of fear. "Baby, no! Remember what Miss Ravenshadow said? We don't open that door, not when night falls!"

But the decision is made, etched into the lines of

Henry's determined jaw. He looks back at us, his Nordic blue eyes a turbulent sea where humor has drowned beneath waves of defiance. "I can't just stand here and do nothing." He declares. "Don't worry, Rosie darling. It will be alright, you'll see." And with that, he wrenches the door open.

NINETEEN

A gust of night air rushes in, cold and unforgiving, clawing at the warmth we had nurtured between these ancient stone walls. It brings with it the scent of death and decay and the whispered threats of things that lurk in the obscured corners of the world. My breath catches in my throat, the taste of danger sharp upon my tongue, a flavor I know will linger long after this midnight ends.

"See, nothing to fear," Henry announces, sparing a glaze at all of us before looking back at the gaping black hole in front of him.

The door swings wide, the silence of anticipation shattering into chaos. There's a heartbeat of stillness, a cruel tease of safety before the night itself seems to surge forward. Henry's back stiffens, his frame outlined in the pale moonlight that dares to creep through the open doorway.

"Something's wrong," I mutter, my voice a ghost in the sudden disruption.

And then it happens. An unseen force, as swift and vicious as a raptor's strike, snatches at Henry. The sound is horrifying, a symphony of tearing fabric and a strangled cry that claws at my insides. He is pulled with such ferocity that his feet barely graze the threshold before he vanishes into the voracious maw of darkness outside. His name dies on my lips; a silent prayer lost to the gaping void where my friend once stood.

For a fraction of a moment, we are all frozen, statues carved from terror and disbelief. Our sanctuary has been breached. Our illusion of control, shattered. Henry, with his sandy blonde hair, Nordic blue eyes, and easy smile, wrenched away like a leaf in a storm. Gone. Just bloody gone. And there's nothing but the echo of that final horrific split second reverberating through my hollow chest.

Then movement, a flash of chestnut hair as Rosie springs into action. Her dark green eyes, usually so full of life, now blaze with a primal desperation. She darts past me, her athletic form cutting through the inertia that binds us.

"Rosie!" I shout, reaching for her, but she's beyond my grasp, propelled by a loyalty that knows no bounds to the boy she loves with all her desecrated heart. The terror that anchors me gives way to awe as I watch the girl I consider to be like a sister to me throw herself into the dangerous embrace of the night. There's no hesitation in her stride, no falter in her step. Rosie is a force unto herself, driven by an unspoken oath, a promise etched into the very marrow of her bones. To love someone that profoundly you'll run straight into the arms of the darkness.

"Henry! I am coming, baby." Her voice breaks through

the heavy air, a clarion call that pierces the veil of fear enveloping us. She disappears into the blackness, swallowed by the hungry shadows that claimed our friend. Her silhouette, a fleeting memory against the backdrop of the unknown, imprints itself upon my mind.

I stand on the precipice of action, caught between the urge to follow and the instinct to seek refuge. The silence left by Rosie's departure is a parasite that eats away at my soul, it echoes with the ghost of her determination. For a long palpitating moment, I stay motionless, my heart a racket against the stillness that now invades the room, but as I flutter ready to chase after Rosie, three sets of arms, belonging to Dean, Oliver and Sam, circle me and hold me back.

"You ain't going anywhere, Sage." Samuel informs me, his grip on me less forgiving than the others. "I will not give consent for them to take you from me." He mumbles so quietly I barely catch his words.

My amber gaze flings to the younger Greyson. "I don't think the shadows beg for permission, Sam, of any kind. They just take whatever they want."

"They still ain't getting you." He growls at me. Samuel speaks like he believes the critters of the night, creeping just beyond the open front door, are here in essence for me alone.

"Sam," I begin to say but my words are cut short as someone behind me breathes, "Close the door." Dean's command, barely above a whisper, carries the weight of our collective fear.

The three engulfing me in their arms let go, and scramble towards the door, joining Luke and Ben. The boys are a flurry of movement, their faces etched with panic lines.

"We have to secure the locks." Oliver adds, his voice unyielding and assertive, but you can just about hear the fright underneath the surface of his façade. Locks click into place, the sound sharp and final in the air thick with dread.

All I do is watch them, my friends, transform before my eyes. Boys who once laughed too loudly over trivial matters now move with purpose, their jovial spirits usurped by survival's grim necessity. Their hands fumble with latches and braces, movements hurried and unsteady, driven by the primal urge to create barriers between us and the horrors we can't see lurking just beyond these walls. My mind struggles to keep pace with reality, every thought anchored to the image of Rosie running headlong into the dead of night. I feel her absence like a wound, raw and hollow, a chasm within that threatens to swallow me whole.

Chaos reigns as many emotions vying for dominance betray any semblance of control we might have claimed. Disbelief grips me, its cold fingers prying at the edges of my composure. The room spins, a vortex of confusion where time stretches and snaps like a rubber band pushed to its limit. The others call out instructions and assurances, their voices distorted as if underwater. I can't seem to find my voice, my tongue heavy with the taste of terror.

"Poppy!" Oliver's hand gripping my shoulder with an urgency that jolts me from my stupor. "Hey, shadow princess, look at me." His hands move to my face, cupping my cheeks and forcing me to meet his gaze. In this action the sleeves of his corduroy overshirt slightly creep down revealing his made by oneself scars on the flesh of his forearms. His meadow green eyes are wide, reflecting the chaos within our sanctuary. "We need to stick together, ok?" He urges, his plea pulling me back to the present, to the immediacy of our plight. Wait, did he just call me shadow princess? That's new. I don't think Oliver has bestowed me with a pet name before.

"Rosie," is all I manage to whisper, the name a testament to the bond we share, to the promise of her return that I cling to despite the shadows that claw at my hope.

"Rosie knows what she's doing." Oliver argues, though his voice betrays the uncertainty that gnaws us all. We're adrift in a sea of fear, the unknown threat outside our doors a siren song that beckons with a sinister allure.

As the last bolt slides into place, the finality of our situation descends upon us like a shroud. We are trapped; the mansion that promised refuge is now a prison. The knocking has ceased, yet its silence is louder than the din of our palpitations. In the oppressive quiet, we stand sentinel, waiting for a sign, for any indication of what comes next in this dark tapestry woven by fate's cruel hand.

"But you all locked the door. How are they supposed to get back in?" My ears are ringing, a high-pitched echo that drowns out everything but the thunderous beat of my own heart. I can feel the tremble in Oliver's hands, which grips my face, and I wonder if he can feel the quake of my bones. Our breaths come fast and shallow, a testament to the terror that has sunk its claws into us.

"Stay close, shadow princess. Just stay close." He adds

more to himself than to me. There's no plan, no certainty, only the instinct to survive that binds us. The world outside has become an abyss, a realm of nightmares made flesh, and we are but fragile vessels amidst the storm.

Once teeming with the warmth of hidden laughter and secrets waiting to be uncovered, the manor around us now seems to breathe with malice. The air is thick and heavy with fear and the iron tang of adrenaline that floods our senses as we huddle together, backs against the cold stone wall. Each creak of its ancient timbers, each whisper of wind through the chinks in the stone, feels like the soft footfalls of death stalking through the halls. Henry and Rosie, those names etched into my blackened heart, now hang like specters in the stillness.

"Should we go after them?" Ben's voice cuts through the silence, desperate and small, a lost child's plea in the darkness. His blue eyes search mine for an answer, for the strength I am far from feeling.

I want to scream, to say yes, to run headlong into the night and snatch them back from whatever hell has claimed them. But Liliana's warning echoes in my mind, a mantra of dread that anchors my feet to the ground. We were told not to open the door. We were told... and yet, splintered by the very thing, we sought to escape.

TWENTY

elter-skelter, a dust devil of chaos and disorder, is brewing inside my head after what happened. My howling thoughts strangle the noises and voices all around me. I feel like drowning in the murky swamp waters, helpless to surge to the surface and break-through for some much needed air. That, or I am being buried alive, six feet under, the weight of the dirt being thrown in the hollow keeping me down, powerless to rise from the grave. What ifs, might haves, could have been if my friends hadn't followed me, on a journey to my gory past, into the baneful maw of a voracious creature with fangs. Four year old me dressed in blood, roaming, all alone, the deserted roads of Transylvania, Louisiana, ought to have betrayed that this wasn't going to end up in anything but in violence porn.

I am sat cross-legged on the bitter cold floorboards, hugging myself around my middle, desperate to reclaim any flicker of control from the clutches of this nightmarish sojourn. I have been staring at the front door for over an hour now, pleading for it to croon with the sound of someone crying out to be let in. The vexed question is would it pulsate by the hands of the people I await for or by the shadows that prey upon us.

The boys haven't stood still for even a New York minute. Ben and Luke have devoted themselves to clearing and cleaning up the kitchen, seeking to distract their minds from the grim fate lurking just beyond the locked doorway. The Greyson brothers and Oliver pace around in the drawing room, without a shadow of a doubt so they can keep an eye on me, since that's the only chamber with a good enough view of the foyer where I find myself. They talk in hushed tones amongst themselves, with fleeting, full of concern, glances my way once and again. Are they fearful that I am going to sneak out and run after our friends, or that something is going to break down the door and grab me, forcefully taking me from them?

"Why me?" I hear Samuel utter in anger, his voice resonating as if someone has their hands over my ears, muffling the sound. "Wouldn't she respond better to your smooth as fuck charms, brother? Or even Oli's akin aura that rivals her own? I am just going to piss her off."

"This once, I don't think flirty and pally would do the trick." Oliver puts forth.

"Sam, look at her." Dean observes. "Poppy needs someone to pull her out of her head, fast, before she suffocates in her dark thoughts, or…"

"Or does something stupid. Yeah, ok, I get it." The younger Greyson cuts in.

"Sometimes you have to be cruel to be kind." Oliver says, as Samuel wends his way towards me.

"Ok, Belladonna, time to get up. Chop, chop. Get your pretty ass out of that floor." Sam tells me in a forbidding tone, his bullish presence looming over me. "Dwelling on what just happen is not going to help us figuring out what to do to get out of this fucking hounding haunt."

I look up at the boy that has planted himself right in front of me, obstructing my view of the front door. He folds his arms over his chest, gazing down at me with his pale blue eyes. "I ain't dwelling, I'm,"

The younger Greyson interrupts me, "Hoping. Belladonna," he pauses, one of his hands moving to massage his forehead as he chews over the words he's itching to say to me but doesn't. Instead, Sam utters, "We should all get some sleep. Let's go find a room."

"Sleep?" I ask, outraged. "Henry and Rosie are out in the shadows, and you want to go to bed? Do you even care?"

"Poppy." The older Greyson hails my name in warning. He and Oliver linger by the threshold between the drawing room and the entrance hall, watching this moment unravel.

"I do fucking care." Sam spits at me. "But they are gone, Belladonna. They ain't coming back."

"Sam." Dean chastises his younger brother this time around.

"You don't know that." I gnash my teeth at his words, rising to my feet.

"Good girl, you're up. Now, to bed with you, start walking."

"You're a dick," I murmur, my voice barely above a whisper, as though afraid to wake the ghosts that undoubtedly linger in the cold stone walls. "God, I hate you." I hiss at Sam.

He chuckles. "No, you don't, Belladonna."

"Ok, time out. I think emotions are running pretty high right now." Luke observes as he and Ben emerge from the kitchen. "We are all tired and a bit disturbed and shaken by the horrid chapter we just endured. Sammy is not wrong, Pops; we need some rest." Please leave it to Luke to try and calm the Soppy storm. That's what Rosie used to call mine and Sam's fights, like a fandom shipping name.

"How about we find rooms at the top? Perhaps the tower. We can watch over the grounds from there." Dean suggests as he strolls to my side, his hand briefly resting on my lower back, a silent promise of protection. Sam nods at his brother's words, his eyes reflecting the flame and his steely resolve.

"Ok," I say under my breath, revolving around and heading up the stairs.

As we climb, the silence presses in on us, punctuated only by the creaking protests of ancient stairs under the burden of modern souls. Despite the sad beauty of the mansion's venerable architecture, it's impossible to ignore the gnawing sensation of dread that coils tighter with each new level we conquer.

"Hey, Poppy, are you alright?" Oliver asks. His steady breathing behind me is the metronome to my racing thoughts, counting out the seconds in a place where time feels irrelevant.

"I'm fine."

Our pace quickens, as if driven by an unspoken

urgency. The stone beneath our feet feels colder now, the air charged with the electric taste of impending doom.

Echoes answer our footsteps, mocking our intrusion into this desolate tower. Something about how the darkness hovers just beyond our sight sets my nerves alight with primal fear. The manor holds its breath, and so do we. Each step forward feels stolen from the grasp of whatever specters watch us with invisible, unblinking eyes.

Oliver's hand brushes mine, a fleeting touch, but it speaks volumes, solidarity, courage, a shared trepidation. Luke's silhouette ahead is rigid, every line of his body tense as though ready to spring into action at the slightest provocation. Ben, dear Benny, tries to mask his worry with a bravado that fools nobody; his humor has no place here among the whispers of the past. And the Greyson brothers, even though at our tailgate, they ushers up, their alpha aura unforgiving and commanding, like executioners leading the prisoners to their harrowing cells, or ghastly gallows.

We are interlopers in a realm of shadows and silence, where even the air seems laced with the threat of violence. We ascend, driven by the need for answers, safety, and anything other than the suffocating embrace of the unknown that creeps in every corner of this forsaken manor.

We crest the final step, and there they are, two rooms awaiting us, sanctuaries perched at the very top of the mansion. My breath catches as we enter, the windows stretch from floor to ceiling, commanding a view that steals the remnants of my unease and replaces them with awe. The vastness of the night sky looms over the slumbering land below, darkness cradling the earth in its silken folds. Yet, despite the beauty, a chill crawls up my spine; an unnerving quality mars this panoramic splendor, the windows do not open. We are observers behind glass, safely distanced yet utterly disconnected from the world outside.

"Me, Sam and Poppy will take this room." Dean announces.

"Yeah, I don't think so, batman. Samuel can bunk with Ben and Luke." I say grudgingly, as I lour at the younger Greyson, my lip curling in a sneer. I am still irked about the way he talked to me before, sue me. "I want Oliver to stay with us." That I vocalize in a dulcet voice. Sam groans but leaves with Ben and Luke, taking the adjoining chamber.

I gravitate towards the window, pressing a hand against the cool surface. The grounds below bathe in pale moonlight, blessing the shadows, who dance across the landscape like silent phantoms playing a grotesque game of hide and seek. My heart throbs with a mix of fear and determination. Rosie... Henry... Are they alive out there, concealed within those shifting shades of gray? Or is Sam right in presuming they are dead? These questions gnaw at me, an itch beneath my skin where I cannot reach and scratch away.

We are bound to this place, tethered to its secrets and sins. A sense of control is what I crave, but the answers I seek seem just beyond grasp, scattered like the stars strewn across the heavens above.

TWENTY-ONE

Adrenaline surges, turning my veins to rivers of fire as I press closer to the barrier separating us from the ominous embrace of night. My breath fogs the glass, so I pass my hand over the blurry patch to clear it up. The obscurity beyond the phantom manor walls harbors an urgency that tugs at my soul, a siren call promising danger and revelation intertwined. The air itself feels heavier here, saturated with the whispers of ancient stone and the weight of history's gaze. My senses sharpen, attuned to the subtlest shift, the faintest breeze that isn't there.

Our fates intertwine with the capricious whims of the unseen in this chamber of vigil and reflection. The darkness outside is a living thing pulsating with secrets it yearns to share. Fingers of fog creep along the ground, ethereal tendrils searching, exploring, as if seeking entry into our sanctuary. And for a moment, I imagine them slithering through the cracks that do not exist, bringing the scent of damp earth and the taste of despair.

I stand rigid, a statue carved from the remnants of trepidation and resolve, gazing into the velvet abyss that stretches beyond the glass. The night's embrace beckons with a beguiling calmness that belies my turmoil, an internal storm mirrored by the tempestuous landscape outside.

"Poppy, about what Sam said," Dean utters, and I chuckle. It took him long enough to try and defend his brother's big mouth.

"Don't worry, batman," I say without taking my eyes from the window and the boundless dark realm beyond it, "I won't be mad at your little brother forever. But you knew that already when you sent him, with his tough love and provocations, to rip me out of my torment. He still ain't sleeping in the same chamber as me tonight, though, much less bed." Suspiring my sorrows and bitterness away, I peer down at my feet before continuing, "I get it; he has faith that Henry and Rosie have fallen victims of crepuscular predators that roam the surrounding bayou. Yet there are ways of speaking your judgment, and then there are Samuel's ways." The younger Greyson's deliverance of his faith was a bit harsh and unpleasant to hear. It felt like a thousand cuts were being ingrained into my flesh. Marry that with his wonted bullyrags and pestering, which usually gets me, well, annoyed but turned on too, and I was just a mess of emotions. "Forgive me for wanting to have a grain of hope that I didn't shepherd my friends to their death."

"Oh, shadow princess, you didn't," Oliver tells me.

While the eldest Greyson brother puts forth, "Henry

took upon himself to open the door, despite Liliana's warnings. Rosie decided to run after him. They were both lucid and sane when making those choices; whatever fate befell after, it's on them, not you. The consequences of their actions aren't your cross to bear, baby."

I turn around to stare at the boys in the room with me. "Y'all are here, in a manor deep in the Transylvania bayou where the fabric of reality has been ripped to shreds allowing unearthly demons to walk amongst us, because of me."

"I fucking knew you were blaming yourself. Don't." Dean speaks harshly, but I can still hear the benign nuance of his words. "You didn't bully us into coming here, we all choose to follow, Poppy."

"Every one of us yearned to be part of your story, of this frayed and tangled web." The boy with somewhat curly medium length light brown hair betrays.

"We're selfish bastards." I knit my eyebrows, confused at the older Greyson's words. "Yes, we are here to help you assemble the broken shards of your evanescent past because we love you. Ohana and all that shit, we are family, no one gets left behind or forgotten, you were never going to do this alone. But we're also here to greedily satisfy our curiosity. That, catwoman, is human nature for you."

I can't fault them for having a curious spirit, isn't that why I am back to where it all started? Yet, I can't let go of this nagging feeling that there's a reason why my brain shut this harrowing episode out. Something's should be left desolate, buried deep in the recesses of our minds.

The boy in a leather jacket, with tousled dark brown hair and piercing blue eyes, hunts for my heed, "Hey, catwoman," coaxing me away from the dark brume in my head, "you are getting lost amid your thoughts again."

"We should never have come." I admit in a hushed tone. "I much rather live in the shadows of a past I don't remember, than forfeit you to whatever hunts out there at midnight."

"You don't mean that, Poppy. You still don't know what you are missing."

"Oliver," I speak his name softly, the rest of my words dying on my lips as his presence materializes right before me like a balm to my disquieted spirit. His hands cup my face in the worshiping and doting way that it's his alone. No one else holds me like that, as if I am the single most dearest thing to them. Our proximity, the eye of the storm where emotions swirl unchecked.

"We've all battled with demons in our past, yours just happen to be of the supernatural kind. We'll figure this shit out, I promise." The boy with a constellation of freckles in his cheeks and nose avows, and I believe him. Lifting one of my hands to his face, I do what I have been dying to do since I met Oliver, tracing the stars that embellish his pale skin with the tip of my fingers.

My gaze goes up from his freckles to his beautiful marriage of hazel and green eyes, dancing between. Oliver's hands drop, his arms encircling me, the embodiment of comfort in a world bereft of certainty. There's no need for more words, his touch speaks volumes, a language of solace inscribed in the gentle pressure of his hands against my waist.

My lips find his, a soft convergence that seeks to siphon strength from our shared vulnerability. He responds in kind, a whisper of a kiss that burgeons into something more profound, a quiet declaration amidst the chaos.

TWENTY-TWO

Mine and Oliver's kiss is like a flower chanting a spring deep soul song. The bud gracefully blooms, at first, a somewhat apprehensive brush of lips, but as the fever settles within, chasing away the chill that dances in the outer edges of our flesh and bones, it deepens, and the petals fan out widely.

In the periphery of this tender moment, my gaze locks with Dean's, those piercing blue eyes that have come to signify both danger and sanctuary. A tacit understanding passes between us; he nods, putting his hands in his leather jacket pockets and revolving around. His silhouette retreats into the shadows as he slips away from the room without protest. The door closes behind him with a peaceful click, like the sealing of a covenant, leaving Oliver and I tangled in the intimacy of half-spoken promises and unvoiced yearnings.

The situation's urgency clings to me, a palpable entity that demands recognition even as I seek refuge in his arms.

Just as our tongues get tangled together within the confines of my mouth, my fingers fumble with cloth, the removal of barriers symbolic of the walls crumbling within us. Fabric whispers to the floor, a testament to the raw desperation that fuels our actions.

"Poppy," Oliver murmurs as his lips split from mine, and I am free to take his t-shirt off. His hesitation flickers across his face, a shadow of concern in his meadow-green eyes as he pulls back. "Are you sure? Aren't you with Dean?" His voice is tinged with uncertainty, the gravity of our tangled emotions hanging between us like a delicate, unspoken covenant.

A smile tugs at the corners of my lips, bittersweet and reassuring. "Yes, but it seems he's okay with it." I reply, my gaze steady. "Can't you see, curly? He left the room to give us some space." I never planned for my guy best friend to be part of this harem my black heart so craves. Still, the older Greyson's understanding is a gift, a silent nod to the complexities of human desire entwined with survival's urgency.

Oliver searches the now empty chamber. The absence of the boy with dark brown hair and blue eyes is like an unsung permission. A sigh escapes him, resignation and longing mingling in the air, and then his hands are on me, urgent and warm. He peels away the layers that separate my skin from his, each garment discarded amplifying the raw vulnerability we both feel, and I finish him off, too, removing his pants and underwear.

The room fades into a blur of moonlight and shadows, leaving only the profound truth of our need. With my palms over his naked chest, I guide Oliver in reverse to the bed, a dance of two souls momentarily untethered from the world's cruel embrace. With a gentle nudge from me, Oliver falls onto the soft expanse of sheets, the fabric cool beneath our heated skin.

The boy, whose beauty reminds that of Timothée Chalamet, gulps, the sound resonating around the room. "Poppy," my name flees his lips like a prayer, but whatever words were meant to follow never come.

"I know." I tell him.

Oliver grimaces as though he just tasted something sour, before questioning, "You do?"

"Hey, don't do that." I say, moving my hands to his pretty face and brushing away the ugly lines. "I will take good care of you. I will make your first time one for the books, ok?"

He nods, almost as if permitting me to fuck him. Well, don't mind if I do. I sink to my knees in front of him, seizing his quite considerable cock in my hand. I mean, I can't even close my hand around it that's how generously cut it fucking is. Lowering my head, I dart my tongue and lick the slit, collecting the salty pre-cum tear in my mouth. Oliver groans, and the sound makes me erect my unusual yellow eyes to his, which appear to be enslaved in the oral black magic I am performing on him.

Without fracturing our eye contact, I open my mouth and take the head in, orbiting my tongue all around it to then release it with a pop. "Rats." Oliver slurs with a hoarse and shaky voice. I giggle, seeing as I haven't really done much here and he is already losing it.

I duly begin sucking him off, bobbing up and down his length, stuffing in more of him in my mouth each time. I use one of my hands at the base to copy the movements of my head. I can feel the self-restraint Oliver is trying to impose on himself, the muscle of his upper thigh feels rigid under my other hand. That won't do, I want him to erupt in mouth. Relocating my hands so they are embedded in his hips, I wolf down every inch of him. Drool drops from my mouth as I seek to keep him deep in my throat for as long as I can.

I start to choke so I know that's my cue to let go. Once I do, one of my hands returns to his cock and begins to beat the meat, while I draw in much needed air into my lungs. "Fuck, shadow princess." Oliver grunts, his upper body plummeting astern to the mattress. His dick swells in my hand, which tells me he's about to climax. I part my lips, arresting his cock back in my mouth, dead on time for his lush bitter nectar to gust all over it. "Rats." He utters again. Jet after gushing jet, I make sure to swallow every last drop of his cum before allowing his dick to leave my mouth. Oliver is still hard even though he just spilled his pearly white seed.

I get up from kneeling between his legs and mount him, a captain taking the helm in a storm-tossed sea, seeking harbor in the disruption of our shared desperation. I grip his dick, lining him up with my dripping wet pussy. Inch by inch impale myself to the brim, feeling the completeness of our union, and begin to move with slow, deliberate rhythms that echo the earth's pulse. The intimacy of our connection, so stark against the backdrop of uncertainty, feels like defiance, a rebellion against the chaos that awaits beyond these walls.

The night presses in, its darkness a shroud woven with threads of danger and the unknown. The phantom manor's ancient stones seem to groan beneath the weight of centuries, their whispers speaking of battles fought and fates sealed within these halls. Our every breath is a challenge to the silence that looms outside, a testament to life's fleeting beauty amidst the ever-present specter of peril.

With each movement atop Oliver, as his dick stretches my inner walls wide, I am acutely aware of the fine line we tread between solace and sorrow, pleasure and pain.

Oliver's touch is a whisper against my skin, a contrast to the tumultuous beat of my heart. His hands, tender and searching, find their way up, tracing the curve of my breast, igniting a trail of fire in their wake. His self-harm scars are on full display, raised and thick tally lines, their hue bleached, soaring up both his forearms from his wrists. I catch my breath, fingers pinching at my nipples, eliciting a soft moan that escapes into the room, a room that feels both sanctuary and prison.

With every push and pull, the slow dance of my hips gains urgency; I'm seeking solace in the rhythm, a rhythm that speaks to the unspoken fears that coil within us. Oliver's grasp tightens, his fingers pressing into my flesh, guiding me down onto him with an enthusiasm that matches the silent screams of my racing thoughts. I quicken the pace, each movement a crescendo of need, a desperate plea for reprieve from the shadows that linger just beyond the walls.

The world around us fades into obscurity, reduced to

nothing but the shared heat between our bodies. The air grows heavy with the scent of our union, a stark reminder of life amidst the encroaching darkness. My vision blurs as I feel that familiar tightening coil deep within, ready to snap.

And then, it shatters.

TWENTY-THREE

I come apart over him, my body clenching around the solid presence that anchors me to this moment. Oliver's name falls from my lips like an invocation as he meets my collapse with his release, his essence flooding into me as he groans my name. For a fleeting instant, we are not just two souls lost within a manor fraught with peril; we are the very embodiment of defiance, clinging to one another while the world outside threatens to break down the door.

I lay my head on his chest, listening to the thunderous beat of his heart beneath my ear. His arms envelop me in an embrace that feels like both a shield and a surrender. The warmth of his body is a fortress against the chill of fear that never truly leaves us.

"Poppy." He whispers, and I know, without even looking into them, that his meadow green eyes are filled with the same tumultuous emotions that storm within me. The night may be ours, but dawn will soon lay claim to the sky, bringing with it the stark light of reality.

Laying here, our breaths mingling in the room's stillness, our chests rise and fall in unison, a silent testament to the life we cling to amidst the shadows that dance upon the haunted mansion walls. It is a fleeting sanctuary, this moment of shared warmth. Still, reality is a relentless pursuer, its cold fingers prying into our cocoon of solace. The ghostly echoes of our past choices whisper through the cracks in the stone, and I can sense the burdens reassembling themselves upon our shoulders, brick by heavy brick.

I turn my head slightly, my raven black hair spilling over Oliver's pale skin, and our eyes lock, a wordless exchange in the dim moonlight. In the depths of his gaze, I find the reflection of my soul, raw and exposed. There's an understanding there, a quiet acknowledgment of the chaos we've traversed and the uncertainty that lies ahead. We are two kindred spirits, momentarily adrift in the eye of a storm, holding onto the sliver of peace we've carved out from the heart of fear. Yet even as our connection deepens, the tendrils of our reality begin to weave their way back around us, a reminder that respite is as fleeting as a dream upon waking.

The room grows colder, the air thick with the scent of foreboding. The manor's ancient stones seem to shift restlessly beneath us, as if they, too, are aware of what lurks beyond these walls. A shiver runs down my spine, and goosebumps rise on my flesh, not from the chill, but from the knowledge that danger permeates every crevice of this cursed place. Our lives hang by a thread, each heartbeat a defiant drumbeat against the silence threatening to engulf us.

"If tonight is all we have," Oliver begins to say, sounding somewhat sad, "I don't want it to end here. Mind going at it again?"

"Oliver Martin Thompson, are you asking if we can have an encore?"

"Perhaps I could take possession of the strings this time. You mostly puppeteered that carnal dance, shadow princess."

I hum at his utterance before proclaiming, "I don't know, curly, you were forcing me down on your cock," I narrow my pussy walls, gripping his sexual organ, which is still stationed deep inside of me, "with a vengeance." Oliver groans, his cock awakening, summoned by my not-so-innocent deed.

"You weren't coming back down fast enough." He notes.

"Is that so? Afraid your dick was going to catch a cold?"

"No. Don't be silly. I didn't want you to be empty for long." That remark makes me laugh despite the source of dread looming in the essence of this God-forsaken place, eager to consume us fully. "So is that a no," the boy with a sprinkle of cute dots on his cheeks and nose doesn't give me time to respond as he spins us around so that I am the one with my back to the mattress. He's on top, "or are you up for me to take control?"

"Well, you are certainly up. What a waste it would be not to go for it. Show me what you got." I tell him, my legs forming a ring around his waist while my arms encircle his neck.

Oliver's mouth descends upon my own, our kiss a soft

brush of lips. His arms, which got trapped between my back and mattress, still bear hug me. And then the magic happens; he begins to move his hips in a riveting way, his pubic bone stroking my bundle of nerves flawlessly. Ok, for someone that just gave his innocence to me, this is some good shit. That entices a moan out of me, but the sound gets disrupted by the entry of his tongue in my mouth the moment my lips part.

Our tongues duel amid lower lips sucking and top lips biting. While our mouths fuck, Oliver, by contrast, makes love to me; he thrusts in and out of my core unhurriedly in a game of forbearing I don't recall consenting to play.

The thought of Oliver loving me isn't outlandish, but it scares me; he treats me as if I am the most beautiful, withered old flower that will crumble to dust by the faintest touch, yet he's the one who may fall apart without much effort. I would hate to be the cause of devastation to his already broken heart and soul. Our friendship was forged in mutual loneliness and inner suffering. At the same time, his depression would urge him to hurt himself; mine would hold me prisoner within my mind, creating a degree of disconnection between me and the rest of the world. Similar tastes just made it easy to be around each other.

I don't know how long we do this, but it feels like sweet torture and bitter pleasure that lasts forever. The knot in the pit of my belly gets tighter and tighter, my orgasm within fucking reach, but rupture just doesn't come.

Migrating my hands higher, I bury my fingers in his light brown curl and pull on the strands until I succeed in making our lips split from one another. "Oliver, I ain't complaining," I so am, "keep edging me, and my wrath will be bestowed upon you, I swear."

"Aww, but your fury belongs to Sam; I wouldn't dare steal that away from him. Nonetheless, please forgive the errors of my ways, mistress." Oliver says, his arms getting out from underneath me as the boy sits on his heels with a swarm of pretty freckles on his face. One of his hands lands on my hip, his nails boring into my flesh, and he resumes his penetration, this time rougher and harder. In contrast, his other hand finds my clit and starts drawing bewitching circles.

Now, that's what I am talking about. "Yes." I moan loudly, let the whole mansion hear me. "Oliver."

What was fruitless for so long is brought to fruition before you can say knife. I come undone, my body going rigid and convulsing uncontrollably. Oliver continues to drive in and out of me, undeterred by the strangling walls of my pussy, dragging my orgasm along as his finger keeps rubbing against my bundle of nerves.

My hands, which were gripping the sheets below me for dear life, crumpling them up real good, fly to Oliver's wrists. I couldn't say what possessed me to do it, but I ran my nails on his skin and scratched away at his scars. I never claimed I wasn't fucked up.

"Fuck, Poppy." He growls under his breath.

His ivy grows in my house of stone, and now I'm covered in him. Blood drips from his open wounds as he fills me with his cum once more. The feel of his warm seed within me and the iron-like scent mingled with the smell of sex that permeates the room force a third rapture to follow the second without an interval in between.

Oliver collapses on top of me, and his grip tightens ever so slightly. His touch is a spark in the darkness, a reminder of the strength we've found in one another's arms. But the night is not our ally; it cloaks our fears and magnifies them, turning whispers into screams and shadows into monsters. We are bound by our shared vulnerability, warriors in a battle where the lines between friend and foe blur into obscurity. And as we steel ourselves for what is to come, I know that this stolen moment of unity will become the armor we don to face the looming onslaught.

TWENTY-FOUR

The silence that follows our given-and-taken rapturous release, as Oliver's body drops to the side and it's no longer crushing my own, is a thick, impenetrable shroud that settles over us with the weight of unspoken promises and shared fears. His voice slices through the stillness, his words wrapping around me like a blanket woven from the threads of worship. "Thank you."

I turn my head to look at the boy beside me before asking, "What are you thanking me for, curly?"

"For seeing me when no one else did. For wanting to be my friend because I am broken and not despite it. But mostly for gracing me with grounds to want to… stay." You can hear the gut-wrenching vulnerability in his spoken words, a testament to the strain we all carry in our bones. "No more self-slaying." He notes, elevating the arm he had draped over my middle and making it hang in the air.

"Oh shit, Oliver," I raise my head slightly to peer down at my belly, which happens to be stained red, "I am so sorry," I utter, my yellow eyes fixating on his bleeding forearm as I brush my fingertips through the dampness there. I made Dean weep blood, too, in our intimate moment. Am I doomed to make my lovers bleed for me?

"You can draw blood from me whenever it pleases you, mistress." My gaze veers to his meadow green eyes, and all I can see ingrained there is adoration and devotion. Fuck, I don't think I deserve this boy.

I lift my upper body from the mattress, using my elbow to keep myself upright and grab hold of his wrist in a way that I hope won't hurt him further. I dart my tongue out and lick his wounds, the sweet metallic taste of gore invading my palate, making me moan.

"Fuck." Oliver says in a muted tone.

I lay back down, mirroring his position on the bed, my hand forsaking Oliver's arm, which falls limp to my hip, as I seize the back of his neck and pull his face to mine. I pause just before our lips meet, allowing our breaths to fade into one another for a moment, and then, shutting my eyes, I kiss him. It's a passionate and possessive kiss on my part, as though I want to devour him. My tongue demands entry into his mouth, parting his lips like there's no more time to waste.

Once our mouths quit each other, Oliver, somewhat breathless, asks, "So what does this mean?" I open my eyes and make contact with his dead-on. "Are we together now?"

"It means that you have a shard of my blackened heart, as does Dean. I want to be with you both. That is, are you okay with sharing?" Neither he nor I say a word for a heartbeat, Oliver, as he reflects on what I have just told him and me as I await his response. Perhaps this conversation should have been held before we had sex. Still, the distress of our dire situation shepherded us to act on our feelings.

"So you would be with me, as well as Dean."

Oliver doesn't word it as a question, but I still answer him, "Yes. I should mention, too, that I have my heart set on three. Don't ask me why, I can't explain it, I just,"

Oliver interrupts my rambling, "Ok."

"Ok?"

"With Dean in the picture, I didn't think I would have a chance. You two are it. I would either have to wait for a breakup that would probably never come or a morbid thought that I don't want to be having about a dear friend for him to die. This is much better." Oliver presents me with a heartfelt smile, so I bestow him with one of my own. "So three, hmmm?"

"Yeah." I assert.

He gives a half-suppressed laugh before announcing, "Sam. He's the third one, right?" I groan because if both of the guys I am with, say Samuel Greyson, there's no running and hiding from what seems crystal clear. I give Oliver an almost imperceptible nod.

"Alright then." He murmurs, his gaze steady and persistent. "I'll take the first shift, watch the window for any signs of Henry and Rosie. You should get some sleep, shadow princess."

"Thank you," I mumble, the words tumbling out in a weary exhale. As I get up from the bed and gather the fabric of my scattered clothing, I ask, "Would you mind getting Dean?" The edges of Oliver's lips curl into a comforting smile.

"Sure." He says, his figure retreating through the doorway, leaving me with the vast darkness outside. Clad once more, I approach the window with trepidation, my gaze searching the moonlit grounds for my friends. But the night reveals nothing save for the unsettling dance of shadows cast by an indifferent moon.

My breath fogs against the glass as I peer into the abyss beyond, each exhalation a ghostly whisper against the pane. The manor's high vantage point offers no solace, only a sweeping view of the encroaching gloom that swallows the land whole. Somewhere out there, amidst the gnarled trees and twisted underbrush, my best friend and Henry navigate a world that has turned hostile, a labyrinth of horror where every step could be their last.

The wind howls a mournful lament that claws at the mansion walls, seeping through cracks and crevices to caress my skin with icy fingers. It speaks of unseen dangers lurking just beyond sight, of evil entities that prowl the darkness, thirsting for fear and flesh. My heart hammers against my ribcage, a frantic drumbeat that echoes the urgency pulsating through the veins of this cursed erection.

Every shadow seems to twist and writhe, animated by dark imaginings, and each rustle of leaves is a conspirator plotting our demise.

TWENTY-FIVE

I stand before the heavy oak table, freshly showered and changed after digging through my suitcase, which still sits by the front door, for something other than the stuff I have been wearing for the past two days. My fingertips graze the ancient grooves in the wood as the morning light filters through the stained-glass windows, casting a mosaic of colors across the room's stone walls. My wet hair, a waterfall of black silk, cascades down my back as I lean forward, my yellow eyes ablaze with resolve. "We can't just sit here," I plea, stretching each syllable like a string pulling us toward action. "Henry and Rosie are out there, alone. Every moment we delay could mean," I swallow hard, a lump forming in my throat, "it could mean we're too late."

I see Dean shift uncomfortably from across the table, his damped hair falling into his piercing blue eyes that now flicker with hesitation. He sighs, the sound echoing off the high ceilings, mixing with the dust motes dancing in the air. "Poppy," he starts, his usual humor absent, "we don't even know what's out there. We've been lucky so far, but luck... it runs out." His comment hangs heavy between us, reminding me of the shadows that lurk beyond our sanctuary, waiting.

Oliver interlaces his fingers together, his meadow green eyes reflecting the weight of our predicament. "It's not just about luck, Dean," he says thoughtfully, pausing to choose his next words carefully, "but certainly we must consider the risks. This manor has protected us, venturing out blindly; it's a gamble against forces we don't understand."

The urgency knots within me; the morning's stillness is deceptive; it whispers of peace when there is none to be had. A shiver crawls up my spine as if icy fingers trace my vertebrae, and the taste of fear lingers bitter on my tongue. We must find them and pierce the heart of this unknown terror that threatens to consume us all. "Can you not feel it?" I implore, my voice a crescendo of desperation. "The silence, it's unnatural. It's as if the air is holding its breath, waiting for the other shoe to drop." I scan their faces, searching for any sign of agreement, but find only the reflection of my dread mirrored back at me.

Dean leans forward, his gaze intense. He's not wearing his leather jacket right now, so when he braces against the cool surface of the table with his extended and very much exposed arms, I get a good eyeful of his veiny forearms and nice biceps. "And what if we walk straight into the beast's jaws? What then, Poppy? We can't fight shadows and whispers."

"Then we face it together," I set forth, the determination in my words steadier than the ground beneath our feet.

Deep down, I know we have no choice; the time to act is slipping through our fingers like grains of sand, and I will not stand by and watch the hourglass empty. "We cannot let fear chain us to these walls while our friends might be suffering. We must be the light that cuts through this darkness."

The heavy silence that has surrounded the room breaks as Luke stands, his presence like a beacon of steady resolve in the storm of our fears. His hazel eyes, usually so full of joy, now carry the weight of unspoken dread, reflecting the gravity of our situation. "We cannot simply remain idle while two of our wander lost and alone out there." The stillness of his hands belies the urgency thrumming beneath his words. Luke is the anchor in our storm, his calm certainty a lifeline thrown into churning waters. "Pops' right." He continues, looking each of us in the eye, one by one, forging a connection that tethers us to the present, the here and now that screams for action. "If we stand together, unite in purpose and heart, what do we truly have to fear?" His gaze lingers on me, a silent plea for understanding, for unity. I feel the gentle pull of his conviction nudging at my unsureness, eroding the walls of doubt brick by brick.

"Think of Rosie and Henry, always the first to lend a hand, to offer a kind word." Ben offers up, his voice a warm blanket wrapping around us, reminding us of shared laughter and moments when darkness seemed nothing more than a passing shadow. "Would they not brave the unknown for any one of us?"

A collective breath is drawn as his words hang suspended in the air, their truth settling over us like the first light of dawn. Luke nods first, a small yet significant gesture that seems to tip the scales. Then Oliver, with a tight jaw that speaks of his internal struggle, and Dean, his stoic face etched with lines of resignation. We are bound by more than friendship; we are a tapestry woven with threads of loyalty and love, too intricate and strong to be undone by fear alone.

A scornful laugh escapes past the younger Greyson's lips. "I think I made my thoughts clear," Sam utters, his tone grave and unforgiving. "They ain't alive, Daisy, and us going into the fucking swamp in search of dead bodies probably means we are next."

"Fine. Let's say they are," I hesitate, my eyes shutting tight and my hands clenching into fists; I can feel my nails boring into the flesh of my palms; that's how badly I don't want to say 'dead,' it hurts too much, "gone." I end up offering, as an alternative, my gaze meeting Samuel's. "Are we just gonna leave their corpses," fuck, I hate this, that tasted foul in my mouth, "out there for the crows to pluck?"

"Goddamnit, Daisy." The younger Greyson exasperatedly exclaims, his hands shooting up to his dark brown hair to pull and tug at the strands. "How the hell am I supposed to say no to you when you look at me like that, with those pleading eyes?" His arms drop to his sides as he gets real close to me and whispers in my ear, "Make me want to die, why won't you, baby." My body tenses as a lustful flutter surges in my gut at the feeling of Sam's warm breath brushing against my skin.

A gust of wind howls outside, rattling the window panes and making me jump away from Sam. It's as though nature itself protests our decision to venture into the bayou and is telling us so. That or something out there doesn't like when the youngest Greyson brother is near me.

With reluctant nods and murmurs of assent, we rise, a phalanx braced against the unknown that awaits beyond the manor's thick stone walls. Our decision feels like a fragile bird in my chest, its wings fluttering against the cage of my ribs, desperate for release.

As we cross the threshold, leaving behind the deceptive safety of the haunted mansion, the world seems to hold its breath. The sky is an expanse of brooding gray, the clouds hanging low and ominous as if bearing witness to our journey. Each step we take is laden with the gravity of our quest; the air itself feels thick with the scent of impending rain and the metallic tang of fear. The swamp looms ahead, a dark maw ready to swallow us whole, its shadows whispering secrets we can't quite grasp.

The dew-laden ground beneath my boots whispers secrets of the night, secrets that cling to the soles of my feet with a chilling insistence. I gaze back at the foreboding silhouette of the manor; it is a fortress of shadows and untold history that has become both our sanctuary and our prison. The footprints before us are like scars upon the earth, leading us toward an unknown outcome. My heart beats an erratic drumming in my chest, resonating with the pulse of the ominous clouds overhead, each step forward a silent prayer for Henry and Rosie's safety.

The cypress trees with their Spanish moss shawls close in around us, their twisted branches clawing at the sky, clawing at us as if trying to warn us to restrain. But we press onward, driven by a burning need to find our missing friends, to reclaim the fragments of our shattered peace. Somewhere, hidden within the heart of this forbidding southern forested wetland, lies the truth of Henry and Rosie's fate, and we are determined to unearth it, no matter the cost.

The phantom manor recedes with each step, and the swamp claims us. We are adrift in a vast sea of ashen browns, navigating crashing waves of shrubs that threaten to trap us in their thorny grasp. The footprints we follow are a lifeline, a path through the chaos, and a harbinger of truths that might shatter us.

The Greysons have been the shepherds of our way through the weeping trees, with Oliver and I behind them and the other two boys at our rear. The swamp seems to breathe around us, exhaling a heavy, musty scent that fills our lungs and fuels our growing unease. Branches snag at our clothes like desperate fingers and leaves rustle with the murmurs of hidden creatures or perhaps something more sinister.

"I would hate for the clock to strike midnight, and you find yourself at the foot of your grave, begging for more time with her." Dean murmurs, his hushed words perhaps only meant for Sam's ears, but the bayou wind carries them over to me. "Don't you see, it's not you or me; we can both end up with Poppy."

"So what, you are willing to share your girlfriend because we might all be about to drop like flies?" Samuel asks.

We are hunters and hunted all at once, seeking answers while bracing for the jaws of an unseen beast. The danger here is a living thing, a pulse that beats in time with our own, a whisper that urges us to flee even as we forge ahead.

"What? No. I am willing to do it because that's what her heart wants."

"To be shared?" Bewilderment stains the younger Greyson's question.

As we press on, our senses are strained to the breaking point, our eyes darting to catch fleeting movements in the periphery, and our ears tuned to the slightest sound that breaks the natural cadence of this place. Oliver angles his head. Hence, his lips are right next to my ear, and he mutters, "Do you think they know we can hear everything they are saying?"

"Three is what her soul seeks; I would rather have a shard of her blackened heart than nothing." The eldest Greyson's brother admits.

"Same," Oliver confesses, one of his hands clasping mine and squeezing tight. Our eyes meet for a short-lived second before returning to the path ahead as benign smiles spawn on our faces.

"Can you please just go and talk to her, Sam?" Dean tells his younger brother, very much out of patience.

"You know, brother, when you said that to me yesterday, I had to sleep in the same room as Luke and Ben. And let me tell you, after Oliver came to get you, there was stuff happening under the sheets of the bed they were sharing?"

"Well, excuse us for wanting to enjoy one another's company while we still can; shit is looking pretty dire," Ben remarks from the back of this string we have created.

"Sammy is just sore that Oliver got some Poppy pussy before he did."

Sam grunts as I turn my face to look at the boy with ash brown hair, uttering in outrage, "Luke!" His response is a shrug married with a devilish smile. I roll my eyes, my head going back to the begrimed imprints.

Once a chaotic tangle of mystery and dread, the footprints unfurl before us like a grim tapestry leading to the inevitable. My breath grows shallow as we breach the tree line, revealing the clearing that hides yesterday's secrets. We have reached our final destination. I guess the time for talk is over; it is too late for Sam and me now.

"Shit," Dean utters as he hastily turns around. "Poppy, baby, don't look." One of his hands comes to the back of my head, his fingers burying themselves in my raven black hair, while his other arm circles me around my shoulders. He pulls my body to him, plastering my face to his chest, almost smothering me, as he seeks to block out my view.

"Dean, what the hell are you doing?" I question, planting my hands flat on his abs to try and push him away. "Let go," I growl.

"Fuck." He yields, and I, before long, wish he hadn't.

The scene laid out before me is a silent scream in the stillness of morning; the bodies of Rosie and Henry sprawl on the muddy ground, motionless, as if the earth has claimed them for its own.

TWENTY-SIX

A cold shiver runs through me, paralyzing my limbs for a heartbeat too long. The air thickens with unsaid prayers, each step towards them an echo of our shared past, of laughter, of whispered confidences under starlit skies. But now, beneath the indifferent gaze of the dawn, they lie like fallen stars, extinguished far too soon. I can feel the others' presence, their horror, a tangible cloud that hangs over us, muffling the sounds of the swamp.

"Rosie." Her name escapes my lips, barely a whisper, yet it slices through the silence like the sharpest of blades. I rush to her side and fall to my knees, the ground damped beneath them, as the world around me narrows to the sight of her pale face against the browns and greens of the soil.

"Baby, I don't think…" Dean begins to say, but gets interrupted by Sam.

"Just let her be, brother."

I cradle her head in my lap, my fingers trembling as they brush a stray lock of chestnut hair from her forehead, searching for any sign of the life that once danced in those dark green eyes. What stares back at me are but blank ashen film over eyes, her soul long departed.

"I fucking hate that I was right." The younger Greyson mumbles, and you can hear the hurt and grief in his words, which are strained with the weight of his suspicions.

Tears betray me, cascading down my cheeks, warm against the chill of fear that tightens around my heart. They fall, unnoticed, onto Rosie's still face as I take in the gruesome tableau. Both she and Henry bear the marks of an unspeakable violence, their throats ripped open, speaking of a blood thirsty predator's embrace. Their bodies, so full of vibrancy just yesterday, now broken and bruised, seem hollow, drained of the blood that once filled their veins.

In the silence that follows, there's a shift in the air, a current of urgency that stirs the leaves around us. The bayou no longer whispers; it roars with a warning, every shadow pregnant with menace. I clutch Rosie closer as if my arms could shield her from the darkness that has already claimed her. It's as though the swamp itself is alive, watching, waiting. The bite, which has become my blurred vision's focus, bares us the insides of our friends' gaping necks. This brutality is a language I cannot fathom, a message written in gore and terror. I hate with all my blackened heart whomever did such a thing. Blood is but a long lost memory on their now pallid skin. Despite that, this crimson hued liquid does not stain the dew-laden ground they rest upon.

The others form a somber circle around me and our fallen friends, their faces etched with disbelief and fear.

"Vampires?" Ben's voice breaks the heavy silence that has descended over the clearing like a shroud. "They can't be, can they?" His words hang suspended, absurd yet terrifying in their implication.

Oliver stands motionless; his gaze locked on what was certainly the coup the grace marrying our friends' necks as if he could unravel this horror with sheer willpower. Luke's hands clench into fists, the knuckles white, his usual bravado stripped away by the rawness of the moment. While the Greyson brothers' eyes bore into me, their concern more so upon the girl with raven's feather hair, porcelain white skin, crimson red lips, and unusual yellow eyes, holding on tight to the dead body of her best friend, willing it to come back to life. To Dean and Sam, whatever predators may lurk in the shadows, waiting to do to us what they did to our friends, are insignificant when weighing up to my woes.

"Are vampires real?" The question echoes in my mind, a fantastical notion that borders on madness. I know we have walked a chamber beneath the out-of-place manor, thronged with relics of once upon a time, tributes to the past of these bloodsucking demons. Deep down we craved them to be just fabricated tales that deceived us into taking these unearthly critters as gospel when they weren't so. Yet, here we stand, cradling evidence of nightmares in our arms.

"There's no refuting it now. Inhuman living things roam the earth with us." Oliver notes, his tone sharp and sober.

"I liked it better when we were in the dark about this."

Dean puts forth, lifting the collar of his worn-out black leather jacket to cover his neck.

As Ben comments, "Maybe a black bear has done it." All of our gazes land on him. "What? They are indigenous to these southern parts of the USA, too."

"Bear attacks on humans are not as frequent as you would think; they are only prone to do it if they feel threatened. Not to mention, black bears would most likely bitch slap you with their front paws, leaving pretty nasty scars on your flesh from their claws, then take a chunk out of you with their teeth." Professor Oliver explains.

"And bears wouldn't relentlessly knock on a door, jerk a person out, and drag their catch into a clearing in the bayou to lay them out like fucking sacrifices." Wait, what? Samuel's words compel me to look through narrowed eyes at my surroundings. He made a pretty good point there; Henry and Rosie's corpses are flawlessly laid to rest in the dead center of this opening in the trees. A sense of foreboding grips me and shakes me to the core. Shit, this is beginning to feel like a trap.

"Ok, a gator then." Ben throws back.

"Benny," Luke lovingly invokes the name of the boy with dirty blonde hair and old-world blue eyes he seems to be very much enamored of. I think it is time you stop with the self-deception. This is the work of vampires, no doubt."

"It doesn't matter," I say abruptly, my voice unsteady and raspy from the quiet tears I wept. "Whodunit or what, wild thing or other-worldly beast, they are still foes. We shouldn't linger." I get up, not bothering to brush off the dirt that befouls my jeans.

"Yeah, Iris is right. Let's go." The younger Greyson asserts as he turns around, ready to abandon the clearing.

"Wait." I pounce on Sam, gripping his bicep to stop him in his retreat. He hisses as though I just burned him with my touch, while his eyes pretty damn quick fall upon my hand, to then shoot up to my own eyes. "What about Henry and Rosie?" I ask, not letting any of that faze me.

"We shouldn't disturb a crime scene," Oliver observes, his voice tense and laced with gravity and anxiety.

As Luke retorts, "What are we to do with two dead bodies? We can't just drive them to the police station, Pops."

"We can't leave them here." I throw back in petulance.

"Poppy," Dean speaks my name with no malice but feels like he finds my utterance lacking.

"Please." I implore. The boys look at me with sad eyes, followed by shared glances. After nodding to a silent conversation between themselves, Sam and Luke carefully lift Rosie and Henry. The weight of their bodies, most likely so much heavier than flesh and bone, laden with the burden of truths too gruesome to comprehend, the sorrow of lives snuffed out too soon. Their limp forms rest in their trembling hands, the finality of death's cold embrace settling upon us all.

As we prepare to carry them back to the manor, a cascade of memories floods me—the laughter and dreams we shared are now cruelly silenced. The pursuit of my past, once a siren's call luring me onward, now whispers deceitful promises. It's a maze of shadows where danger lurks, eager to claim more victims.

"We gotta go," I murmur, my voice barely a whisper

against the mounting dread. "We need to leave this place." The others pause, their eyes finding mine, seeking an anchor in the storm of uncertainty. "This manor, my past, it's not worth it. Not at the cost of your lives, our lives." My words falter, but the conviction behind them burns fierce and unyielding. The truth is a sharp and clear blade cutting through the fog of confusion.

The air around us is thick with the scent of moss and decay, the bayou closing in like a dark cathedral, its arches crafted from twisted branches that seem to reach us with gnarled fingers. Shadows play tricks on our eyes, and every rustle of leaves carries the weight of a thousand unseen threats. The atmosphere is charged with an urgency that propels us, driving us to flee from the horrors that have stained this sacred ground. As we move, the sense of being hunted presses close, the darkness a living entity that breathes down our necks, whispering of dangers yet to come.

TWENTY-SEVEN

The air is thick with mist and sorrow, mourning for the two lives hanging limp in Sam and Luke's arms. My heart hammers against my ribcage; each beat is a visceral reminder of the fragility of our human existence. We probably should have left their corpses in the clearing, but I couldn't forsake them once more, even though all we bring with us is Henry and Rosie's flesh and bones, their vitality long gone.

Henry Caldwell, once so vibrant and full of laughter, is now silent forever; it's a truth too harsh to accept. Henry, the boy with sandy blonde hair and bright Nordic blue eyes, the captain of our university basketball team, has an appetite that rivals that of gluttony, the sin itself. Who's going to steal and eat all of our food now? Henry, my steadfast jokester, why did the light in your eyes have to dim on such an unforgiving night?

Rosie Blackwood, the Enid to my Wednesday, had a spirit of adventure that could only be extinguished by death. Rosie, the girl with shoulder-length chestnut hair always in a practical ponytail, with dark green eyes and sun-kissed skin, the captain of the track team and our cheerleader, always ready with a smile that could light up the darkest hole any of us found ourselves upon. For those who think I am the glue that holds this group of outsiders in tandem, that isn't true; Rosie was the one who brought us together and kept us from ever separating. What will happen now that she's no more?

I suck in a breath, trying to find strength in the bond we all shared, but it's like grasping at smoke, there's nothing substantial to hold onto. "Keep moving!" Sam's voice cuts through my grief, sharp and commanding. Yet even he can't hide the tremble that belies his fear or the breathlessness from carrying the bridal-style Rosie in his arms.

We reach the cars, a supposed haven, only to be greeted by the cruel sight of rubber strewn across the gravel, tires slashed to ribbons. Panic surges, icy and suffocating, as the stark realization hits us: we are truly stranded. There will be no quick escape, no roaring engines to transport us away from this unfolding night-mare. Vulnerability wraps around us like a shroud, cold and unyielding. The shadows of the towering phantom manor walls mock our desperation, whispering secrets of our impending doom. We are alone, abandoned by fate, and left at the mercy of whatever malevolence lurks within the unseen depths of the surrounding swamp.

I don't understand why would my soul seek to come back here. Why would I feel a pull straight to Doom's embrace? My heart whispers in my sleep that I ran away from something, but it wasn't what dressed me in blood in the bayou. I don't even think I am here to listen back to my past; I am here for them, those three looming shadows from my dreams, dark wisps that called to me so lustily I couldn't hear reason. It's their fault.

"Damn it!" Dean's curse slices through the bleak silence, echoing the dread coiling in my gut. The vulnerability of our group, exposed under the pale morning light, is palpable, a tangible thing that we can almost touch. The safety we took for granted has been snatched away, leaving us naked to the dangers that await. The weight of our friends' bodies in our arms is a grim reminder of what could be in store for us should we fail to act.

"Everyone inside, now!" The younger Greyson growls. Our survival instincts kick in, raw and primal, as we return to the mansion, the only shelter available in this desolate landscape. We are prey, and the hunter is closing in.

The hallowed echo of our footsteps reverberates against the ancient stone as we stumble into the haunted mansion's cavernous embrace. Its cold indifference starkly contrasts the warmth that once emanated from Rosie and Henry, now nothing more than silent figures cradled in Sam and Luke's trembling arms. The kitchen, with its long table that had hosted laughter and stories just days before, now serves as a sad altar for our fallen companions. We lay them down gently, their pale faces reflecting the scant light filtering through the begrimed windows. This tableau of despair, Rosie with her usually bright green eyes now dull and lifeless, Henry's infectious smile forever stilled, etches itself into my memory, a cruel memento of our predicament.

"FUCK!" Samuel howls, his outburst making us all jump.

"They slashed our tires." Luke points out.

"More like ripping them to pieces, no tire left." Oliver corrects the boys with ash brown hair.

"Look at this... just look at what's happened to them." Ben's voice cuts through the thick silence, sharp with thinly veiled panic. I think he's in shock. "We are cut off and shut in from everyone and everything. That's us in a few hours." He declares, pointing at Rosie and Henry. A cacophony of voices rises, each of us frantically casting about for some semblance of hope, some strategy to defy the darkness closing in on us.

"We just need a plan. We can't just stand here waiting for whatever did this to come back!" the older Greyson insists, his usually calm demeanor frayed at the edges.

"Right, because sitting ducks is exactly what we are without transport." Sam grits out between clenched teeth, his frustration manifesting in a restless energy that has him pacing like a caged animal.

"Then let's not be sitting ducks," I interject my voice, a mixture of dread and defiance. "We have to do something."

"Like what, Poppy? We have no idea what's out there!" Samuel counters, his hands gesturing wildly, knocking over a glass that shatters against the stone floor, the sound a sharp exclamation point to our fraught nerves. I step back from the younger Greyson, my back crashing into Dean's front. His arms come around my middle as if he seeks to protect me from monsters that roam the bayou and his brother's fit of rage. I wouldn't say I like it when Sam calls me by my name.

"Samuel, calm the fuck down." A beat of silence follows, heavy with the weight of unspoken fears, before Dean speaks again, his tone resigned yet resolute. "We fortify this place the best we can, using what daylight we have left. It's all we can do."

"Fortify with what?" Luke scoffs. "Our bare hands? Good luck with that."

"Better than running headlong into danger," Ben replies, his gaze steely. "We need to think this through, consider every option."

"Options? Our options died along with them." I gesture toward Rosie and Henry, the sting of tears threatening as the reality of their stillness hits me anew. "We can't afford to wait for a miracle, Ben. We have to make our way out."

"Let's just... let's just run for it."

TWENTY-EIGHT

"Let's just... let's just run for it." Luke's voice slices through the oppressive atmosphere like a beacon of resolve. He is standing by the window, the light casting long shadows across the sharp angles of his face. "The same road we came in on, it's risky, but it's our best shot. We know that path; we can navigate it, even if it means facing the unknown."

I pause, considering the suggestion, the image of the road unwinding before us in my mind's eye. Dean's arms tighten around me as Oliver's hand clasps my own, both boys seeking to give me solace and strength for what's to come.

"Eight hours." Oliver murmurs beside me, drawing my attention away from the haunting memories. His meadow green eyes are clouded with concern, reflecting the dappled sunlight that struggles through the ancient glass panes. "That's all the daylight we have left. If darkness falls before we reach safety..." His voice trails off, leaving the grim implication hanging in the air like a shroud.

"Eight hours." I echo, tasting the truth of his words. There's an undercurrent of fear there, one that resonates deeply with my own. That's enough time to get to the main road I walked upon many moons ago. The beaten path may be our lifeline, but it's also a gauntlet that we must run, with the specter of night looming over us, threatening to swallow us whole. "Ok," I say, my voice scraping out from a throat tight with emotion, "it's a risk, I know." My eyes lock onto Sam's for some reason, perhaps searching for that flicker of resolve I've come to rely on. "But staying here isn't just standing still; it's giving up. We can't let fear paralyze us." The truth of my words resonates through my ribcage's hollow chamber. "We owe it to them," I nod toward our fallen friends, "to try, right?"

My heart beats a steady drumroll, echoing the urgency that trembles in each word. There are no guarantees on that road; the same shadows that danced at the edge of our vision on the way in will be lurking, waiting. But hope is a strange, fragile, yet unyielding creature that refuses to die quietly within me.

"Dammit, this is insane," Sam's voice cuts through my reverie like a knife through the silence, low and rough with barely contained anger. He turns away from the group, his broad shoulders tense as he stares down at the corpses of Rosie and Henry, his jaw clenched. A string of curses spills from his lips, muttered under his breath but audible enough to carry the sharp edges of his frustration.

"Insane or not, we don't have a choice." I insist, slipping away from his older brother's embrace and letting go of Oliver's hand so I can turn to face Samuel. His hands ball into fists at his sides, the knuckles white with the effort to contain the storm brewing inside him. I draw near him carefully and gradually, as though the younger Greyson is a frightened, wounded stray that I desperately want to help but might bite or scratch me if my approach is too sudden. I wouldn't mind either from him, but that's off the subject. "You think I don't feel it, too? The anger, the loss?" My voice rises slightly, not in challenge but in solidarity. "But we honor them by fighting, by surviving. What else can we do?" I conclude as I am at last at his side.

Sam's pale blue eyes meet mine, and in them, I see the reflection of my turmoil, a storm of grief and determination. For a moment, we stand in silent communion, two souls bound together amid chaos, united by a shared conviction that to give in to despair would be the final betrayal of all we hold dear.

I sweep my gaze over the group, their faces etched with panic and sorrow. Rosie and Henry's still forms remind us of our grim reality. We are lost in a landscape of horror, each breath haunted by the specter of death that lingers close.

"We should bury them." My yellow eyes return to the boy with dark brown hair, a shade darker than his older brother's, at his out-there and unexpected reflection.

"Hmmm, Sammy, we don't have time for that," Luke observes.

"Foxglove." His eyes bore into mine, imploring me to follow this unreasonable idea. When I don't answer him immediately, he says, "Fine, I don't need you anyway." Sam says to me in a harsh and grating voice, shifting his focus to the dead bodies laid out on the oak table. "I will bury them myself as you guys gather whatever we need." He utters as he begins to pick Rosie up.

The younger Greyson seemed to have misread my momentary muteness but was preaching to the choir with his comment. "Like hell, you are doing it alone, mister," I tell him, finally breaking this tongue-tied spell I found myself under. With Rosie in his arms, he looks back at me, a grateful smile painting his face, while I nod, thankful for the semblance of control that the task offers.

"You two are out of your damn minds." Ben puts forth. "Like Luke said, there's no time for dilly-dally here. And we can't just take it upon ourselves to put them in a hole in the ground. What if someone asks for them?"

"Right, a mother that showed more love to her clients than her daughter, spending every penny they had on pills rather than food, or parents that never fucking bothered to call or check up on their son the second he got emancipated from them. Are you telling me those people are going to care now when they didn't give a fuck when their kids were alive?" Sam's words cut deep, but they are the sad gospel of our friends' lives. "Their family is gathered here, in this kitchen, in this manor, in this southern hellhole of a town. I say we give them a proper burial rather than leaving them to rot on a kitchen table."

"Alright, brother. But I will help you instead of Poppy. I don't want her out there where peril awaits."

"What? No. I want to do this with Samuel." I say in response to Dean's behest.

He glares at me with furrowed brows and follows my words, with my pet name slipping from his lips in an imposing and unforgiving manner, "Catwoman."

"Try and stop me, batman, I dare you."

The eldest Greyson's brother groans. "Fine. You get whatever time it takes us to harvest supplies; after that, we have to go. And if something happens to her, baby brother," Dean addresses Sam, pointing a finger at him, "I will kill you myself."

"Noted. Come on, Foxglove." Samuel nods toward the grand gothic-style French doors that lead from the kitchen to the mansion's backyard.

Once outside, as the bitterly cold breeze brushes against my skin, making some of my black strands wing their way to my face, apprehension ultimately catches up to me. This is a reckless thing to do.

"I am sure I saw some shovels lying around by the wrought iron fence of the graveyard." Wait, is there a cemetery in this place? "And before you ask, there's not much to it, some old ass stone coffins being devoured by withered poison ivy and a bunch of broken headstones. Probably why you didn't notice it before." Wow, did Samuel Greyson gaze into my thoughts or something? Not beautifully creepy at all. "I happen to stumble upon it when I came out for a wander around the grounds as you and," he clears his throat of whatever distasteful thing lodged itself in there before continuing, "Rosie reposed in the drawing room, and the others delved more so inside the mansion. Now, Foxglove, you go get me a shovel while I put Rosie down by a good spot to bury them and go back inside for Henry."

Usually, I push back whenever the younger Greyson orders me around. Still, the clock is ticking away at us, so I reply, "Sure."

"Good girl," Samuel tells my retreating form, a lewd itch blooming within me at his praise. How inappropriate and inconvenient since this is by no means the time or place to feel like that, and I can't scratch it either. Ugh, I hate him for making me feel this way.

It doesn't take me long to retrieve the shovel and rejoin the boy with almost black hair and pale blue eyes. Both Henry and Rosie's dead bodies lie in wait at his feet to be buried.

"Ok, I will dig; you keep an eye out." A grimace graces my facial features at his curt instructions. "Don't look at me like that, Foxglove; we both know it will be done quicker if I do it."

Oh, that's it; I am done not biting back. "Because you are a man," I say, crossing my arms under my chest and lifting an eyebrow.

"I ain't getting myself in that hole, so I plead the 5th," Sam utters, shoving the shade in the dirt and standing on the step to dig deeper. After scooping up and disposing of quite a bit of soil, he asks, "How hollow do you think I should go?"

"I don't think it matters, to be honest. This is the bayou; on the next downpour, they will probably rise to the surface either way." New Orleans is a town built upon reclaimed swampland and very much below sea level, resulting in a high water table in the soil. Long story short, shit moves around a lot below ground, and to ward off nasty surprises popping up like flowers, folks from the crescent city bury their dead above ground. I know we are a bit farther up than the big easy, and I don't mean it just in Louisiana, but the town of Transylvania is still rooted in a swamp. Oliver is not the only one with out-of-the-hat facts.

"Then why, my deadly flower, am I doing this if they are just going to spring up from the grave like zombies?" He asks in anger.

"Hey, don't snap at me, mister. You are the one that said we should bury them." I point out.

"God, I hate you." The youngest Greyson's brother growls.

"No, you don't. You love me." I remark.

Sam opens his mouth, about to respond, but a gust of air rushes past us in a hurry, intruding on our moment. It brings the scent of decay and the iron tang of long-dried blood and chants in a hushed tone, "Poppy."

"Did you hear that?" I inspect the tree line, searching for the source of these eerie happenings when my eyes spot something. "Is that a mausoleum crypt peeking from in between the trees?" You can just about perceive it, hiding in the shadows cast by the cypress and willow trees, with its weeping old granite stones, dead dried-up poison ivy and thorny rose vines that consume its walls, and its gaping mouth silenced by rusty black iron bars.

His gaze hunts for what I laid eyes upon; once Sam sees it, he replies, "Yeah, it seems so. But we ain't going in there."

"Why not?"

"Foxglove, here we are in the open; we can at least see shit coming, make a run for it, and with a stroke of luck, make it back inside without dying." It's cute that he thinks we can outrun whatever stalks these grounds. "There," Sam points at the mausoleum, "anything can onslaught from anywhere; we will never see it coming, not until it's too late."

"Poppy." Something whispers again, compelling my gaze to return to the charnel house. I squint my eyes, as I am sure I see three dark silhouettes within its confinement, and begin walking in its direction.

"Poppy!" Sam shouts my name, making birds fly in frightened haste from the trees. Something falls to the ground, the shovel, I presume, as he rushes to my side and grabs me by the elbow, forcefully halting me in my tread.

I peer at the boy who ruffles my feathers more often than not. "Please don't call me that," I ask of him.

"Don't call you by your name?" His hand starts cascading down my arm until it reaches my hand, and he clasps it desperately and vigorously. The younger Greyson's touch stirs something within me; it awakens a lustful hunger that only he can sate.

"No." I purr, our eyes latching on to one another. "I prefer it when you call me by anything but my name."

He chuckles. "Ok, Foxglove. Can you maybe not dawdle that close to the trees?" The intensity of our stare at this moment makes something growl amidst the trees, which causes Sam and me to split up.

"Hmmm, Sam, I don't think you have to carry on digging."

"Why?" His question is spoken with an unsmiling and harsh tone as he seeks to mask its slight tremble from either thrill or terror.

"Because there's two open graves right there."

TWENTY-NINE

"What?... The fuck." Sam hisses in utter disbelief. Unseen behind an old stone coffin with its lid cracked in three, the shards dropping inward, are two already drugged-up holes awaiting their forever residents. We proceed towards them with an uneasy feeling in the pit of our stomachs.

"On the bright side, there aren't eight holes. Now, that would be peculiarly eerie." I remark in an attempt to break the tension that is engraving itself at the moment.

Sam levels a sly glance my way with an arched eyebrow. "I," he rolls his eyes, huffing and puffing, "don't even know how to respond to that. Let's get Henry and Rosie and be done with this."

As the younger Greyson goes to retrieve our fallen friends, my eyes return to the mausoleum. My cadaverous pallor must betray an aura of foreboding, almost as though I sense a disquieting metamorphosis. An invisible thread binds me to something that paces within and keeps on roughly tugging at their end, seeking to lure me right into their arms. I seem to find myself in this duel between needing to stay rooted to my spot and wanting to walk right in there and jump the bones that rest inside.

Fingers grasp me by the chin, pulling my face away from the charnel house and compelling my gaze to fall upon Samuel's pale blue eyes. Worried lines grace his sharp, handsome features. "What's wrong?"

"Where did you go?" He asks, his voice is gentle yet firm. You can't miss the deep concern those words convey.

"What do you mean? I haven't moved." As I speak those words, streaks of dirt somewhat beautify Sam's skin and clothes. I peer at hollows in the ground, with great difficulty since the younger Greyson's grip on my chin is unrelenting and unforgiving, to find them filled up. "I don't understand. Was I lost?"

"Yeah, kind of." He raises his other hand and places a finger on my forehead. "Up here." Sam remarks. His hands move in chorus; the one on my chin drops to my throat as his other brushes some of my black strands back and settles in the back of my head. "You kept saying Thorn, Kol, and Orpheus. What do those words mean?"

"I… don't know," I answer in a low tone.

His eyes dance between mine, searching for something in their amber depths. "I am still unsure how I feel about this whole sharing thing." He puts forth.

This conversation has been going on for a long time; I don't think this is the moment to have it. The sand on our hourglass is pretty much all at the bottom; soon, there will be no more grains left to fall. We should be heading back inside. We should be running away from this God-forsaken place, never looking back, before we end up exactly like Henry and Rosie.

"Sam," My voicing of his name ends in a squeak as the hand on my throat squeezes, cutting off my supply of air.

"Here's the thing, Hemlock. I don't share well." He points out right as the hand on my hair clenches into a fist around my strands and pulls unceremoniously. "And I tend to break my toys. Just ask my brother."

"I'm already broken, Sam."

"Yeah, aren't we all? Tell you what," The younger Greyson utters, tugging my body right against his with the hold he has on my throat, getting my face a breath away from his. "I will give you a taste now, and if we get out of this alive, you and I, we can have a feast."

"Samuel Greyson, are you telling me you want to participate in my harem?" I taunt the poor bastard.

"Well, I love my brother. And I guess I don't mind that loser you call a best friend. We all have been deprived of quite a bit in our pathetic excuse for a life, and seeing how shit can end just like that, in the snap of some devilish fingers, I would hate lamenting something I could've had if I wasn't such a sour possessive bastard consumed by greed and envy."

"So," I drag the word out, awaiting him to confirm or deny his position on this.

"I will be in your little harem, but I might brush over the fact that you are dating the other two. In my head, you are only mine."

"So, what you are saying is if I want a threesome, I should go to your brother and Oliver. Got it." I tease him.

He groans and does his utmost to choke me, bullying

me into parting my lips in a futile attempt to gasp some air into my lungs. That's when his lips collide with mine, making our teeth crash with the abruptness and violence of this action. While the kisses with his brother are prudent and gallant on his part, yet still crammed with desire, and the ones from the boy with tiny stars smeared across his face are a sweet love poem written with every soft brush of our lips, Samuel's are savagely dominating and ferociously covetous, putting to shame my downright reign over Oliver's mouth. I may wield the scepter with Oliver, and Dean and I share the crown, but Sam sits on the fucking throne, and the only spot I can take it's his lap.

Our backdrop feels heavy, vibrating with an aura of disfavor and vexation that isn't coming from either me or Sam, as though the trees themselves and whatever dark story hides in their shadows do not wish us together. Despite that, we press on, screw what might be sulking and lurking within the swamp.

His mouth is driving me batshit crazy with lust. His tongue punishingly penetrates my mouth with no finesse or subtlety; he shoves it as deep as he can get it to capture my own then and suck it into his mouth.

The hand on my hair disentangles itself from my rat nest, made so that way by all the pulling and tugging, it comes to the valley of my breasts and begins to travel down my body, only skimming my clothes with its finger-tips, stopping just above the waistline of my black skinny jeans. I make out the sound of a button being unclasped and a zipper being lowered, swiftly followed by his hand reaching into my pants and panties. Sam's fingers hunt out what they are looking for with no hiccups, immediately setting about rubbing my bundle of nerves.

My moan gets swallowed by his mouth on mine, his kiss not easily dispelled. It doesn't help that his other hand hasn't lessened its grip on my throat, keeping my head and my body exactly where my very tall boy, with dark brown hair that marries well with his fair skin, wants it, bang on at his mercy.

His fingers move up and down my folds now, parting them, smearing and gathering my juices, his intent obvious. I bite his lower lip hard, perhaps a bit too strenuously. "You ain't sinking those dirty fingers in me, mister," I inform him, my voice a beacon of strictness, as I lick my lips, tasting the tangy metallic flavor upon them from the blood I drew from the younger Greyson.

When Sam opens his eyes, his pupils are dilated, so much so that there is only a slight ring of pale blue around the now black eyes. "Do you want to come or not?" I whimper because I do, I am dying to cum. "Thought so. You can clean that pussy later."

"Samuel!" I call out his name in ill humor. Look, I am no lady; regardless, I still have some standards; pardon me for not wanting scum to end up inside my vagina.

"Ugh, fine." He groans but removes his fingers from my pants, which makes me melt once more. "Damn, there is no pleasing you, is there, my deadly flower?" He slips two of his fingers in his mouth and licks them clean. Promptly after they are out, whatever smut he removed from them gets spit back to where it belongs: the ground. I don't know if I should feel repulsed or aroused by this. That's the thing about Sam; he, in every respect, brings out a spectacle of conflicting emotions within me. And who has time to decipher my feelings for Samuel bloody Greyson? Not me. Time is very much against us. "Now, Hemlock, where were we?"

"You were about to finish me off, mister," I tell him.

He tosses a twisted and wicked smirk my way as his hand goes back inside my pants, diving into my underwear, his fingers getting themselves right by the gate of pleasure between my legs. Sam's lips draw near mine at the same time that the tips of his fingers press in against my core. "Let me hear you purr like a kitten, Hemlock." The younger Greyson demands before his lips cover mine.

His tongue enters my mouth as his fingers bury themselves inside my pussy. In and out, they both go in a delicious rhythm that very quickly satisfies the hungry monster, which finds itself in knots in my belly.

"Your cunt feels so fucking warm." Samuel fractures the kiss just long enough to inform me, his tongue going back to playing with mine straight away.

I can't believe I am being fingered by Sam right next to Henry and Rosie's grave; how perverse of us.

"And you are so wet, my deadly flower; look at how effortlessly my fingers slide in and out of you." He breaks off the kiss once more, but his lips don't return to mine this time.

His nails dig into the flesh of my neck, and I can feel a slight tremble coming from his hand as it constricts around my throat. It's funny, and I sense my legs begin to shake. At the same time, the rest of me locks up and goes rigid, yet the boy fucking me with his fingers seems to be the tense one, like he is seeking to establish some self-control of some kind, holding himself back.

"That's it, devour my fingers, Hemlock," Sam says to me, his fingers thrusting into me, well, as best as he can with the restriction my clothes impose, but vigorously nonetheless.

"Yes, Sam." I purr.

"Open your eyes, baby; I want those yellow eyes on me when you come." I do as I am told, and our gazes collide. His fingers root themselves deep within my core and arch, hitting that riveting spot inside our pussies.

"Oh my God, Sam." I whimper as I fall apart, and just before my vision goes white for a few seconds, either caused by the intensity of my orgasm or Sam strangling me, I notice something dire behind him.

"God, hmmm?" He chuckles.

"No. " I am still getting hit by crashing waves from my rapture, my walls narrowing on his fingers, "sure." It's hard to get words out when you can't fucking breathe. "But Sam, look. The iron gate from the mausoleum is wide open."

The world around us seems to take on this dull hue, as the sky above is painted gray with wrathful clouds. Tick-tock goes the clock. That's when we hear it: the rustling of leaves and the snap of a branch coming from amidst the darkness.

THIRTY

"Fucking finally," Dean utters as Sam and I barge through the gothic French doors into the phantom manor hand in hand. Immediately upon hearing the soft click of the doors shutting behind us, I revolve my head to gaze at the yard beyond, the glass fogging up thanks to my heavy breathing. Even in the thick of the condensation, I can perceive that nothing has chased after us.

"If y'all were ready to leave, why didn't you shout for us?" Sam asks his brother.

"You two seemed otherwise engaged when I went out there to fetch you. I could've interrupted your little moment, but you two needed that." Dean remarks that his tone is somewhat bitter but still caring. "I guess this means you are a part of this thing Oliver and I have with Poppy, then?"

The younger Greyson grunts, his hand squeezing mine quite hard. "Samuel blatantly ignores the part where I am also dating you two," I reply.

A half-suppressed laugh flees past Dean's lips before he comments, "Of course he is; my baby brother doesn't share well. Fool's paradise, I suppose, but hey, you got the girl; why so blue? Is it because your balls are still blue?" I follow Dean's gaze, which happens to be leveled with Sam's crotch. Hold and behold, someone's cock is straining against the confinements of his jeans. Holy effing cow, he's packing something big down there.

"I had a boner for Poppy for the good part of three years now; what's a few more hours until we are out of this nightmare? At least my deadly flower got to bloom in my hands." Samuel points out. Our gazes fall upon one another as he lifts two of his fingers to his lips, inserting them in his mouth and sucking on them. Wait, those were the ones that were inside of me; he's gulping down my juices.

The kitchen is deserted apart from the eldest Greyson's brother. "Where's everyone else?" I stray from Sam's pale blue eyes and the venereous moment there. At my words, the other boys make their way into the kitchen, their voices echoing with a messy web of unease and agitation.

"Did you two fucking have fun out there? It's not like time is slipping by right through our fingers." Ben spits at us.

"Benny," Luke says in a honeyed voice, planting his hand on Ben's shoulder, attempting to soothe the slender boy with dirty blonde hair. "Sorry guys, he's a bit on edge."

"And can someone tell Oliver he cannot take that bloody book with him?" Ben says, full of dark clouds, gesturing towards the boy with a face graced by a constellation of freckles clutching with both arms, close to his chest, the of yore pages we brought up from the chamber below this very mansion.

"We can't let this trip be for nothing. We can't let Henry and Rosie's death be in vain. This book is heavy with lore, about supernatural creatures that should be fictional but ain't, about this shrouded in obscurity place," Oliver pauses in his speech, his meadow green eyes migrating to me, "about Poppy's past." His knuckles turn white from his dead grip on that old tome. "I am not leaving this much knowledge behind."

"If Oliver wants to carry that weight with him, then let him, Ben." The younger Greyson sets forth, his words firm and final.

"Fine. Can we go." Ben suspires, his tone yielding and tired.

"Let's not forget water," Dean says, his voice a beacon of calm in the eye of our storm. "We'll need to stay hydrated out there." It's a simple statement, but it carries the weight of survival, grounding me momentarily in the practicality of his foresight.

With a dark gray layer upon the sky, the kitchen is a chaotic splash of subdued daylight and shadows. Still, we find what we are looking for: bottles of water lined up like soldiers ready for battle. My fingers fumble with the lids, screwing them tight, ensuring that not a single precious drop will be lost to carelessness. The others join in, their movements brisk and focused, as if preparing these small vessels can shield us from the nightmares that breathe down our necks. I can hear the collective shudder of adrenaline coursing through us, a symphony of anxiety and resolve that pulses just beneath the surface of our skin.

We gather the bottles close, stuffing them into bags, pockets, and anywhere they fit. Our hands shake with the chill of the phantom manor's unforgiving stone and the terror that resurges within us, griping us with its harrowing claws, now that we are on our way out of this bane. I dare say that deep down, none of us itched to do this; that might be why we have been procrastinating, putting off the inevitable conclusion. We knew time was fleeting, yet we still wasted it. I don't think we have enough.

"Ok, time to go hell for leather, people." I urge, my voice barely above a whisper, though it sounds thunderous in the silence that claws at the room's edges. It's an uncomfortable truth, the urgency that propels us, the understanding that time is a luxury we no longer possess. We must escape this place, escape the darkness that threatens to swallow us whole.

Water weighs heavy in our hands as we skid to a stop at the entrance, the ancient door looming before us, an unwelcome barrier between the somewhat known and the unfathomable. With trembling hands, I reach out, fingers grazing the cold, iron handle. With one final, collective heave, we burst from the haunted mansion's suffocating embrace, the echo of our haste a ghostly chorus in the barren halls. The resounding wood boom against stone as the door closes behind us is a sad toll, marking the end of refuge and the beginning of an odyssey across perils untold. My breath comes in jagged gasps, drawing the damp, musty air into my lungs that burn with exertion.

"It's now or never, gang," Luke announces. That's

when the urgency seizes us completely, a palpable force that sets our nerves alight, and we hit the road, sally forth on our run.

The silence outside is a void, chilling and profound. It hangs over us like a shroud, the stillness so complete it feels like a living entity, watching, waiting. Distant leaves whisper secrets to the wind, a calm reminder that life persists beyond our dread. Our breaths are ragged intruders in this mute world; each exhales a foggy testament to the fear that claws at our insides. We stand, a small band of survivors on the threshold of the unknown, the weight of our decisions anchoring us momentarily to the spot where safety once was promised.

Shadows cling to the corners of my vision as I scan the treacherous path ahead, a narrow ribbon threading between an ocean of encroaching darkness. The sun, a treacherous ally, casts its dying light through the clouds across the swamp, turning trees into twisted sentinels that line our escape. In the quiet, every snapped twig is a thunderclap, every rustling leaf a siren's call luring us into the arms of unseen horrors. We know in our bones that the sanctuary of daylight is fleeting and that every heartbeat brings the night's terrors closer.

Why does it feel different? When Sam and I were in the back of the manor, I knew something malignant crept on us, haunting us just beyond the cypress trees with their Spanish moss mourning veils and the willows with their dropping branches in an eternal weep. Yet, I didn't feel the fright that I do now coursing through my veins.

Time, once a passive stream, now rushes past us like a raging torrent, each second slipping through my fingers like grains of sand. With every thunderous beat of my heart, I feel the pulse of urgency thrumming in my veins, an insistent drum calling us to flight. My legs move of their own accord, muscles burning with the effort of our frantic pace. Beside me, Luke's breaths come in sharp bursts, his presence a beacon of steadfast resolve that pierces the haze of my fear.

The path unwinds before us, a serpentine challenge that tests the limits of our endurance. Each step is a battle, fought on the uneven ground that seems eager to claim us, to draw us down into its unforgiving embrace. "Everyone take heed of where you tread. Please." Dean's steady voice cuts through the chaos, his words a lifeline anchoring me to the moment and the task. We cannot afford to stumble, to falter, not when every tick of the clock is a harbinger of the darkness that awaits to swallow us whole.

I can taste the metallic tang of adrenaline on my tongue, a bitter elixir that fuels my determination. Oliver runs beside me, the book rooted within his backpack, unequivocally pressing down on his shoulders, straining his back. The boy with messy light brown curls is a silent specter whose grace belies the terror we all share. His eyes, wide and glistening, reflect the golden hues of a sun that betrays us with its retreat. We are bound by an unspoken pact, a collective will to survive that knits our disparate souls together.

As the road unfurls its treacherous length, the shadows stretch out like grasping fingers, eager to pull us into their murky depths. The air grows thick with the scent of decay, a foreboding aroma that clings to the back of my throat. Branches claw at the sky, their silhouettes etched against the dimming light. The underbrush rustles with the movement of unseen creatures, their intentions as obscure as the path ahead. Our footfalls are a desperate rhythm, a staccato beat punctuating the oppressive silence enveloping us. We are chased not only by the horrors of the manor we left behind but also by the unknown perils that lie in wait, eager to claim us in the dark.

The sun, a once radiant orb in the sky, now bleeds its last streams of light into the horizon, laying a carpet of elongated shadows across the path we tread. The aches in my body are deep, each step echoing the one before, reverberating through bones and ligaments. Hope tugs at my heart, fragile as a spider's silk thread, while fear wraps around my mind like a shroud. We must outpace the darkness; it is a relentless pursuer, indifferent to our human fragility.

As dusk tightens its grip, the world transforms into a canvas of stark contrasts and urgent whispers. Our breaths rise in plumes, mingling with the mist that creeps from the underbrush, tentacles reaching out to pull us back. Branches snap beneath our hurried steps, the sharp crackling sounds like gunfire in the silence of the impending night.

THIRTY-ONE

The world blurs past me, a vortex of shadow and fear as we flee down the darkened, beaten path that seems to stretch endlessly under the cloak of dusk. My breath comes in ragged gasps, each a heavy weight in my chest, fighting against the tightness that constricts my lungs. My heart pounds a frantic rhythm, syncopated with our footsteps hammering against the gravel, a desperate percussion filling our flight's silence. The cold air bites at my skin, but I barely feel it through the adrenaline that courses like wildfire through my veins.

"You need to keep walking, Poppy, straight into town. If mummy gets taken, just run and find someone to help." The echo is back, a ghost that seems to plague my mind and haunt these hellish swampy grounds. The mystery of my past, once a silent whisper, now screams in my ears as we run from unknown but deeply felt dangers. Not only can I hear her desperate voice once more, but I can see the imprint of that moment being played back by pockets of smoke within the scarred fabric of reality. My thoughts swirl chaotically, a storm of what the hell, and am I conjuring this up, or is this an apparition? I don't think the others can see it, so this must be an evocation on my part.

It's the woman from the painting. Her black hair cascades down her back, swaying to a sorrowful chant sung by the bayou breeze and her hurried steps. Her stunning crimson-red gown drags behind her, staining the hem with smut. Her eyes, like amber flames, shift between the road ahead, the tree line, and the little girl at her rear. The child's tiny hand clasps that of the woman for dear life as, just like us, they flee from something.

The abandoned phantom manor of my fragmented memories looms in my mind's eye, its ancient stones a silent sentinel to the chaos of my life. Yet even with the urgency that propels us forward, a melancholic ache settles in my bones, a longing for something that seems as elusive as the darkness that chases us. The further we get, the stronger this pull gets, that invisible thread bounding me to shadows within this God-forsaken place, straining more and more doom to snap sooner or later. Or so one would think? I don't understand why something deep in my soul would be telling me to turn back, to return.

The apparition speaks again, "May they forgive me for not being able to keep you safe until you were of age and they could claim you." What could she possibly mean by that?

In the thickening gloom, every shape takes on a sinister form and each rustling leaf whispers of lurking threats. Our bodies are pushed beyond their limits, muscles screaming and fibers straining with the exertion of sustained terror. My legs move mechanically, driven by sheer willpower as if they belong to someone else, someone who hasn't spent their life running towards enigmas, only to find oneself fleeing from nightmares. We are all reaching the brink of our endurance, the physical manifestation of our collective dread etched in the lines of exhaustion that mark our faces. My companions' eyes reflect the same haunting fatigue that weighs down my limbs. But we cannot stop; we dare not stop. The darkness behind us is too thick with peril, the unknown too fraught with danger.

Our hands seek each other, finding solace in the contact, a silent vow to face whatever comes together. Mine grasps Sam's, and we become one another's lifeline amidst the chaos as we all press onward, deeper into the woods where the twilight grows ever more oppressive. The trees stand like sentinels, their branches clawing at the sky. At the same time, the wind howls through their leaves and layers of Spanish moss, carrying with it the scent of our fear and the promise of oblivion.

Every shadow teems with potential horror, every snap of a twig underfoot a portent of doom. The bayou envelops us; its embrace is suffocating, and its whispers are malevolent. We are hunted, prey in an ancient game whose rules we do not know, whose stakes are our very lives.

How are we not at the main road yet? It didn't seem like this much of a country mile when we did it by car. The beaten path unfurls like a serpent beneath our feet, black and fucking endless. In the shroud of nightfall, our breaths are ragged symphonies; each inhales sharp with fear and exhales a whisper of fading hope. We run, muscles burning with the effort, hearts pounding against our ribs so fiercely it seems they might break free. Our very beings ache with the strain, but there is no solace in rest, not when every shadow may conceal a predator.

Luke's presence is a constant at my side, and the rhythm of his strides is a counterpoint to my own. His confidence, usually a beacon in our darkest times, now wavers like a flame under the assault of the stormy night. Even as I draw strength from his unwavering loyalty, I cannot shake the feeling that something unseen watches us, biding its time before it strikes.

And then, in a heartbeat, the world tilts on its axis.

"Luke!" The name tears from my throat as he is ripped from my side, an anguished cry piercing the oppressive silence of the bayou. He is there one moment, a solid presence next to me, and the next, he is gone, swallowed by the insatiable maw of darkness. My mind reels, unable to process the sudden absence, the void where he stood moments before.

His scream slices through the air, a razor-edged harbinger of terror that chills my blood and sears itself into my memory. But his wail is not unchaperoned; married with it comes her voice, "Run, Poppy, run," as her ghost is snatched from reality, much like Luke just has.

"Poppy, do not linger. We have to keep going," Dean utters, the terror in his voice undisguised, as his front meets my back, and one of his arms comes around my middle so he can drag me along with him. The older

Greyson's words slash me open, but I know he's right. If we stay rooted, we are making it easier for these things to catch us.

As Dean and I spin around so we are no longer stumbling backward, I hear the echo of Luke's pain and determination intertwined, a testament to his unyielding spirit even in the face of unimaginable fear. It propels us forward, a desperate surge of adrenaline fueling our legs as we sprint through the gumbo that seeks to gobble up our feet. Each step upon the mire is like the bayou reading us our last rites.

Luke Alexander, the nurturer of lost souls, the ungrudging, selfless, and kind young man who would put everyone else's needs and wishes in the heavens before his own. Who's going to calm the raging storms now? Luke, the boy with ash brown hair, hazel eyes, and tanned skin, was always in baggy workout clothes, covering up his athletic physique. Shit, I am going to miss the parade of gray sweatpants. Shit, I will never know now how many pairs that boy owned? Luke, death has laid hold of you way too soon, but I guess you get to be reunited with your dear mama toot sweet.

I will never be able to shake the image of Luke's terrified eyes, their silent plea forever haunting me with each frantic beat of my as good as the dead heart. We are prey, stalked by shadows that feast on fear, and my mind recoils at the reality, clawing at our heels.

The older Greyson shoves me towards his brother, who takes my hand back in his. I must've let go of it when the clock struck midnight, and the shadows turned into the killers we feared them to be. "Don't ever let go again, Tulip," Sam grunts at me, his grip on my hand mercilessly firm. The younger Greyson's touch is reassuring and a stark reminder of our vulnerability.

"We need to keep moving." Ben gasps, and I nod even though every muscle screams in protest.

"Poppy, stay close." Dean breathes, his voice a trembling thread amidst the cacophony of our distress. Oliver's strong hand finds mine in the dark, a solid counterpoint to my terror. We are bound by desperation, an unlikely constellation hurtling through the night. The forest seems to close in around us, a living entity aware of our plight, its breath heavy with the scent of moss and menace.

The darkness is alive, writhing with secrets too terrible to name. Spanish moss dangles before us like spider webs, ready to capture us in their embrace. Branch snatch at our clothes with skeletal fingers, and the unseen foes that claimed Luke linger just beyond the reach of our senses, a specter waiting to strike again.

Samuel's hand tightens around mine, fingers digging into flesh as if he could somehow anchor us both to life itself. "Whatever happens," his voice cuts through the thick air, a whisper fraying at the edges, "I mean it, Tulip, please don't fucking let go."

Every shadow becomes a threat, and each rustle leaves a potential harbinger of doom. Our breaths come in ragged bursts, white puffs in the chilling air, and the very earth beneath our feet feels like it could give way at any moment, plunging us into an abyss from which there is no return. We weave through the cypress trees and their shawls of Spanish moss, a dance macabre choreographed by the primal urge to survive.

"Right there, do you see it?" Oliver's urgent whisper slices through the gloom, his words sharp needles of alarm. My gaze follows his pointing finger, but I see nothing beyond the oppressive blackness that swallows our path.

THIRTY-TWO

Mummy is gone, but she told me to run, so I am doing that. I can't say I know where I am going; I haven't been outside our home, well, ever. And after Mummy got swallowed by the shadows, I hared off straight into the swamp, abandoning the beaten track. I had faith that if the ashen-faced trees could hide them, they could eclipse me. Oh, how will-o'-the-wisp of a four-year-old me.

I think back to when I went to play on the cemetery grounds, and Mummy got so mad. That's the day she unfolded the gospel that things are lurking in the bayou that intruded upon our family's sacred grounds to hunt us down and bring our bloodline to an end. They came the very moment I was born as if summoned by the rise of this poppy flower bud. Mummy said that the sole reason they have been able to keep them at bay was thanks to Liliana's help, she enchanted the stone walls we live upon to keep me safe and sound, but even her magic wasn't strong enough to stop the bale from coming knocking at our door.

I stumble and fall, my tiny body almost getting wolfed down by the gumbo that graces the ground I have been treading upon. The stench of death and the sharp tang of sickeningly sweet metallic smell invades my nostrils. Wait, oh my God, my body isn't submerged in mire; it's blood, and there is lots of it. As I crawl out of the shallow puddle, I peer behind me, and my yellow eyes grasp what has brought about my fall.

"Daddy." I sob. His ashen complexion rivals the trees around us and the cloudy sky above. Broken bones protrude from everywhere; there are gashes all over his limp body, the worst being the one in his belly, his bowels spilling out through three deep tears, as though done by sharp claws. "Mummy told you not to open the door. You should've listened, Daddy."

I feel something fracture within my brain; one second, I am weeping and mourning not only my fallen Daddy but my vanishing Mummy; the next, I am a little girl dressed in blood, numb, totally dissociated from what just took place. My eyes are dry as I get up from the ground and begin walking away from the nightmare that eluded my mind until today.

"Oh my God," I falter as I wake up from my reverie, only to find myself in a similar night terror, "the lady in the painting is my mother." I breathe. The night air clings to my skin, heavy with the scent of impending rain and the burden of escape. With each breath I desperately seek to draw in, I suck in the dampness, my lungs filling with the promise of life beyond this cursed bayou.

"What?" Samuel's question comes out forced and

choked, either from shock caused by my out-of-the-blue betrayal or simply from the exertion of running.

The lights of the small town flicker in the distance; tiny beacons of hope pierce through the shroud of darkness that has enveloped us since we fled. Like stars fallen to earth, they guide our forlorn flight towards salvation. I can almost taste the freedom that awaits us there, still far away but inching ever closer with every stride.

"I think I am Queen Roseverden and King Alexander's lost daughter."

"What?" The swamp echoes with everyone's howl.

My feet pound against the bayou floor, the rhythm a haunting sound to the chaos of my thoughts. Sam's breaths come in ragged gasps beside me while Dean's determined grunt punctuates the night. We are a group of shadows fleeing from a past that claws at our heels, seeking to drag us back into its depths. The town's lights grow brighter and more insistent now, and with them, there is the possibility of a future unmarred by the horrors that chase us. Yet even as hope swells within my chest, it is fragile, threatened to be crushed by the unknown's weight lurking just beyond sight.

"Wait, Poppy, weren't they slaughtered by…"

Oliver never gets to finish his observation as the older Greyson interrupts. "We'll discuss that when we claim sanctuary beyond this damned place on earth."

The night air is a chilling caress, clinging to my skin with the tenacity of shadows that refuse to be left behind. Our breaths are visible puffs in the cold as we hurtle through the underbrush, and for a fleeting moment, I find an odd comfort in their ghostly dance. It's a silent testament to our existence, as if to say, despite everything, we are still here.

Oliver's presence is a gentle hum beside me, his empathy always like a beacon in this suffocating darkness, while Ben's quietness next to him speaks of the hurt he must be feeling after witnessing the person he cared very much for being snatched away by unseen hands, devoured by darkness itself. His resilience and guts to swallow it all down and carry on without Luke is invigorating. As for the Greysons, their steadiness is the anchor that keeps us all from drifting into despair. The small town lights beckon us with the warmth of a hearth fire, promising shelter from the relentless and ruthless storm coming down on our lives. But hope is a delicate bird in my chest, its wings fluttering against a cage of ribs too frail to protect it.

"Almost there," I whisper more to myself than the others, but chaos erupts before the words settle into the crisp night air.

A guttural sound pierces the silence, a monstrous symphony composed of snapping branches and unearthly growls. I feel the ground shudder as something immense moves with terrifying speed through the darkness. Then, in one heart-stopping moment, Oliver and Ben are ripped from our side, their forms enveloped in a haze of black that seems to swallow them whole. Their screams, raw, visceral sounds that tear through the fabric of the night are etched into my memory, echoing in my ears long after they've been silenced.

"No!" I scream. That one word is a prayer. I hope someone answers.

"Run!" Oliver's voice, ragged with terror, rings out, a stark command that splinters my blackened heart even as my legs obey. Or it could be that the only reason why I stir is due to Sam yanking violently on our clasped hands. The cry from the boy, whose face is beautified by a cluster of stars, is a clarion call, urging me to move, to survive, even as part of me dies with the sound of his pain. The bayou has claimed them, dragging them into an abyss I cannot follow, leaving behind only their echoes and the haunting laceration of their absence.

Benjamin Foster, the Grumpy to my Snow White, particularly in the morning without his caffeine fix, found all the flaws in our stupid shit but still went along for the wild ride. Ben, the boy with dirty blonde hair, old-world blue eyes, and an unyielding faith in this found family. Benny, the scared little boy who disguised his disquiet with dark humor, who had to bear the cross of a condemning and punishing God during his early years, to die at the hands of hellish demons now. How can fate be so cruel?

Oliver Martin Thompson, I want to make an analogy here with Wednesday Addams and one of her boys, but Oliver is too unique for that; neither Tyler nor Xavier can't rival any of my boys. Oliver, my boy, had medium-length light brown hair and cute curls that any girl would die for. I wish I had pinned a bunch of bijou flowers on his hair; how whimsical would that have looked? Beautiful meadow green eyes, nose, and cheeks graced with my favorite constellation. Oliver, my best friend, was the only person I fell in with with the same dead-ringer tastes as me. Who is going to tell me out-of-the-blue ghost stories, out-of-the-hat Louisiana facts, or watch morbid crap with me?

Panic grips me, fierce and unyielding, as if the darkness itself has hands, and it means to pull me down next. My breath comes in sharp stabs, tearing at my throat, each inhale an insult to the stillness of the void that has claimed my friends and one of my lovers. The cypress trees blur into a streaked tapestry of horror painted in shades of fear and adrenaline. It's a race now, a desperate bid against creatures made of nightmare and malice. And all I can do is run, propelled by Oliver's final word, a plea wrapped in anguish that I dare not ignore.

My legs, pistons fueled by pure terror, churn beneath me, Sam's labored breathing to my left, Dean's shadowy figure cutting through the underbrush to my right. The world has narrowed to this single imperative, run, just fucking run. My heart hammers against my ribs, a frantic metronome keeping time with our flight. Each breath is a sharp dagger of cold air in my lungs, and every step forward is a small victory against the encroaching dark that threatens to consume us.

The eldest Greyson brother glances back, his eyes a stormy blue that once laughed under sunlit skies now are wide with fear. "Baby, I know it hurts." Dean is not talking about the ache in my legs or lungs from the running; it's about Oliver being gone. He's right; it fucking hurts; it feels like a shard of my heart is missing. Oliver took it with him; how dare he? "We just have to keep moving." He gasps, voice edged with desperation. Sam nods, his usually contemplative gaze hardening with determination as we push ourselves beyond exhaustion, beyond thought.

There's an unspoken bond between us now, a pact forged in the fires of shared horror, whether we survive together or not.

Our footfalls are a staccato rhythm against the bayou floor, a frenetic dance with death hot on our heels. Strings of Spanish moss and branches whip at my face, leaving stinging fire lines in their wake. The darkness is alive, an evil entity that breathes down our necks, its icy fingers brushing the nape of my neck with every glance backward. My mind races with the possibilities of what might be lurking just beyond sight, ready to snatch us away as it did Oliver and Ben and Luke before them.

"Keep close!" The older Greyson shouts over the din of our escape, but the thickening air strangles his voice. The shadows pulse and twist around us like the night is a living, writhing thing. With each stride, I feel the weight of their absence, a void that aches in my chest, a hollow echo where once there was warmth and camaraderie. But there's no time to mourn, no space for grief, only the primal need to outrun the darkness that seeks to claim us next.

Ahead, the lights of the town flicker like distant stars, beacons of hope amidst the suffocating gloom. We're close to safety, yet miles stretch before us. The air grows denser, charged with electricity, as if the night is gathering its strength for one final assault. And in that moment, I understand with chilling clarity that it is not just about reaching the light; it's about escaping the all-consuming darkness that hungers for us, always just one faltering step behind.

THIRTY-THREE

The night is a shroud, tight around our shoulders as we flee through its unyielding grasp. The leaden clouds have cleared somewhat to reveal a thin crescent moon hanging in the sky like a silver sickle, reaping darkness instead of the light we crave, barely illuminating the path ahead. Each breath I draw feels heavy, laden with the damp chill of the air and the weight of unknown fears snapping at our heels.

Sam's hand in mine is a tangible reminder that I am not alone in this abyss of shadows, but it's not enough; I need more, so I hunt for his older brother with my other one. Dean's rapid breaths are a syncopated rhythm to our flight as our fingers intertwine. The Greyson brothers are the sole reason I am still running, fleeing, seeking to survive this night terror. The distant lights of the town flicker, beacons of hope wavering in the murky distance. We run, our feet pounding against the earth, a desperate litany against time.

A gasp tears from Dean's lips, a sharp sound that slices

through my pulse pounding. His fingers tremble within my grasp, slipping away as an unseen force wrenches at him. "Poppy!" He cries out, and his voice is tinged with terror, a stark contrast to the calm steadiness that usually defines him. His gaze locks onto mine, wide blue eyes reflecting a silent plea, the intellectual resolve crumbling under raw panic. I tighten my grip, trying to anchor him to my side, but it's like clutching at smoke.

"Dean!" I shout the name, a desperate incantation against the dread that claws at my chest. But the darkness is greedy and devours my words, leaving only the echo of fear behind. He stumbles backward, pulled by an invisible tide, the shock etched into his features, betraying our reality's sudden fragility. I lunge, reaching for him, but my fingers are close to empty air. The force that claims him is relentless, pulling him away as easily as the wind carries autumn leaves. The older Greyson's form becomes a silhouette, a ghostly figure receding into the abyss. Then he is gone, swallowed by the void that separates us.

Dean Greyson, forever the protector, my knight in shining black armor, rode into my life in a black ZR10R motorcycle. Who is going to rescue me now? Dean, my boy with tousled dark brown hair, piercing blue eyes, and just enough ink to make a girl like me drool. Dean, my mouth, my alluring winged parasite, the one person who could fly through my darkness and root out the speck of light. Who is going to find me when I am lost? A fucking black moth, how prophetic of his mortality? Shit, who is going to stop Sam and I from killing each other? We need a buffer. We need Dean.

I can barely breathe. This can't be happening. I can't…

I feel a pull on my other side.

Oh God, please don't. I can't lose them both. I can't lose everyone.

Samuel, his fingers, once interlocked with mine in a grip I thought unbreakable, begin to slip away, one by one, as if pried by the hands of fate itself. "No, no, no, not you too," I whisper, a mere wisp of sound carried off by the cruel winds. "You told me not to let go. Don't you dare fucking let go, Sam."

The younger Greyson fights against the pull, his body tense as a bowstring. I see the strain in his arms as he reaches for me, his pale blue eyes wide with the shock of betrayal, not by me, but by the very world that seems to be ripping him away from safety, from sanity. The maddening charm that usually dances in those depths is extinguished, replaced by stark terror. There's a desperation in his grasp, a plea for solace in a reality that offers none.

Our fingertips brush, a touch as brief as a falling star, while he says in a muted tone, "I'm sorry. I love you, my carnation." And then he is torn from me, just as Dean was, disappearing into the unknown that hungrily claims all we hold dear.

"I love you too." I lament into the void Sam has left, letting the bayou breeze drag those words away into the nothingness that embraces me.

Rooted to the spot, I turn, my head whipping from side to side. This fog manifests out of the shadows, a living thing, a silent predator that wraps its cold tendrils around me, obscuring my vision. My eyes are wide, their yellow irises darting frantically for any sign of my lover. But there's nothing, only the impenetrable gray that devours shapes, light, hope. I squint, my gaze piercing through the murk, searching for anything. A shadow, a silhouette, a glimmer of the life that was just beside me moments ago. My heart is a drumbeat of dread, each thump screaming their names in a rhythm of loss and despair.

Samuel Greyson was the thorn in my side, the one who loved to hate me and hated to love me. His persistent bad mood and ill-temper could put Ben's crankiness to shame; the younger Greyson is the bate king, and that's for sure. Who is going to piss me off now? Sam, my boy, had dark brown hair, a hue darker than his older brother's, almost black, with pale blue eyes, and was as tall as the ashen bark trees surrounding me. I was looking forward to being one of the toys he breaks, mostly because I wanted to see him try. Who is going to break me now? We wasted so much bloody time fighting when we could have been fucking.

The darkness is absolute, a void where even the distant lights of the town seem like a mockery, a dream too far to reach. It's as though the night has swallowed them whole, leaving no trace of Dean or Sam, my lovers, my protectors, my anchors in this nightmarish sea I feel like I am drowning upon. With each second that stretches into eternity, the reality of their absence is a weight on my chest, heavier than the enveloping fog, heavier than the world.

The mist, once a mere whisper in the night, now billows into a thick shroud that clings to my skin with clammy fingers. It swirls, a dance of ghostly veils. I stand at its mercy, disoriented, the path we had taken swallowed whole by its voracious appetite. Each breath I draw feels heavy, as if the air is saturated with the essence of this ethereal enigma. The world around me has contracted into a sphere of a few fleeting feet, beyond which lies a canvas painted in shades of nothingness.

"Dean? Sam?" My voice is a tremulous thread, fraying as it weaves through the dense curtain of fog. It echoes back to me, a hollow sound mocking my isolation. I strain to hear a response, a sign of life. Still, only the oppressive silence presses against my eardrums like an unwelcome confidant whispering tales of solitude.

My heart races, each beat a frantic drummer summoning the courage I so desperately cling to. The cold tendrils of the fog coil tighter, a serpent constricting its prey, and I am lost within its embrace, alone, abandoned, adrift in a sea of uncertainty. Where the figures of the Greyson brothers once stood, there is now only the chilling absence of their presence. In this moment, the truth slices through the haze; they are all gone, torn from my grasp by forces unseen, leaving me as the last sentinel in a world where light dares not tread.

"Dean! Sam!" The urgency claws its way up my throat, and my cry cuts through the darkness, a beacon of raw desperation. "Please. Don't leave me." I reach out into the void, half-expecting to feel the solidity of their hands in mine, but my palms are close to emptiness. "No!" I howl. The reality of their disappearance settles like lead within my chest, a despair threatening to suffocate me as much as the fog itself. Shadows flit at the edge of my vision, phantoms or perhaps memories, playing a cruel game of hide and seek with my mind.

My pulse thrums with a primal terror, the intuitive knowledge that something hunts us in this purgatory. The air is thick with the scent of damp earth and the unspoken dread that lingers like a foul perfume. Every nerve ending screams for me to flee, to escape the clutches of whatever malevolence has claimed everyone I open my blackened heart for. But my feet are rooted, as though the ground itself has decided my fate, to wait, to listen, to face the horror that slithers beyond sight. The darkness whispers to me, a sinister lullaby. I know that within its depths lurk answers I may wish never to uncover.

THIRTY-FOUR

The mist advances like a living entity, coiling around the Cypress trees with serpentine grace. It is as if the bayou itself exhales a breath of secrets long kept, shrouding the world in an opaque embrace. From within this spectral veil, they emerge, one moment mere phantoms at the periphery of my vision, the next solidifying into forms of arresting beauty. As I remember from stories whispered in the darkness, they belong to night and nightmare, their presence an unsettling blend of allure and terror. The delicate features of their faces are marred by streaks of red, a macabre adornment to their pale visages. I stand rooted in place, captivated and repulsed in equal measure.

My blackened heart drums a staccato rhythm against my ribs, betraying the primal part of me that knows fear as an old friend. As our gazes lock, theirs are wells of abyssal depth, pulling me into a dance of mortal peril and enthralling mystery. Curiosity blossoms like a night-blooming flower in the pit of my stomach, its petals unfurling with each thudding heartbeat. Fear still laces through me, cold and sharp as a blade, yet there is a warmth to my wonder, a heat that rises to combat the chill. What might it mean that these creatures of darkness seek me out, their eyes reflecting moonlight and something else, something deeper?

The swamp breathes around me, exhaling a damp mist that clings to my skin like the touch of a ghost. They advance, these figures of shadow and blood, their feet barely disturbing the carpet of gumbo as they glide closer. My pulse thrums in my ears, a frenetic symphony accompanying their approach. "We have found you, our queen." They intone together, their voices woven into the night fabric, resonating with a power that seems to stir the air. The words fall upon me, heavy with an otherworldly gravity yet carrying a strange comfort, a whisper from the depths of a dream I cannot quite recall.

In the echo of their declaration, time stretches thin, fraying at the edges as memories claw their way through the smog of my fractured mind. There is a tug, insistent and gentle, on the frayed cords of my soul. An age-old summons stirs within me, a call that has lingered in the marrow of my bones pretty quietly until this very moment. Silent but not dormant, I have been feeling remnants of this invisible thread for a while now; that's what dragged me here to this God-forsaken place in the entrails of Transylvania, Louisiana. These beautiful demons are the ones on the other end, pulling, reeling me in like a fucking fish caught on a hook on the back of a fishing line.

Recognition flickers, distant and elusive like the memory of a past life or the relic of a lullaby once heard in the embrace of slumber. Could these beings, these elegant nightmares, have always been a part of me? A piece of a puzzle I never knew was incomplete?

Suddenly, the world sharpens into crystal clarity, each leaf, each whisper of wind, each drop of crimson on their alabaster skin. The sense of recognition swells, filling my chest with a storm of emotions that threatens to wolf me down. Danger hums in the air, a dissonant melody played on the strings of the unknown. These creatures, eyes like an endless night, beckon me toward a gospel shrouded in darkness. Still, it is my truth, calling out to the core of my being with a voice that rumbles like thunder over a trembling land. I stand on the precipice, and below me, the hellish abyss awaits, its secrets veiled in shadow. Yet, amid the terror, there is the pull of destiny, irresistible and inevitable, drawing me closer to the edge.

The cursed bayou around me stills as if holding its breath. I find myself trapped by an unexpected serenity; the fear that once clawed at my insides, threatening to spill out in a scream, ebbs away like the tide withdrawing from the shore. In its place, a tranquil stillness settles deep within my soul. These spectral beings before me, their existence woven from shadow and starlight, seem not harbingers of doom but of destiny. They stand, timeless and patient, as though the world itself bends to the gravity of their purpose. And inexplicably, amid the chaos of my thoughts, I feel the sweet, sorrowful ache of homecoming.

I cannot fathom why my pulse steadies at their proximity nor why my heart, which should be drumming a frantic rhythm of flight, chants a soothing melody instead. It is as though I have wandered through a life cloaked in mist, the path unclear, only to emerge into a clearing where everything aligns. My eyes meet theirs, these enigmatic guardians of night. Within those abyssal depths, I see a reverence that pierces the veil of my confusion, hinting at answers to questions whispered in dreams.

With each step they take toward me, the air grows dense, charged with the weight of unspoken histories. Their eyes are lanterns in the dark, illuminating not the path ahead but the path within, casting light on the fragments of memory that dance at the edge of my consciousness. Anticipation coils in my stomach, not the jittery nerves of uncertainty, but the profound eagerness of a door creaking open after centuries sealed shut. And though the penetrating gaze of my nocturnal courtiers promises a journey fraught with peril, I am drawn to the precipice of revelation, for within their silent promise lies the allure of understanding the enigma of my existence.

Compelled by a force beyond my understanding, my hand lifts of its own accord. The air between us crackles with the promise of secrets long buried, my trembling fingers an inch from one of the spectral beauties before me. They seem woven from the very fabric of the night, their luminous forms shimmering like stars caught in a mortal coil. I can feel the pulse of old magic in my veins, thrumming to the rhythm of a timeless song I have known but never had the pleasure of hearing.

My breath catches as my skin grazes his; it is less touch and more like a merging of essences, a whisper of contact that speaks of unity and separation all at once. There's a familiarity in the caress of his ghostly flesh, a remembrance of a bond forged in the crucible of creation.

Tears well in my eyes, not from fear but from the profound realization that these beings are part of the puzzle that is my very existence. How can one feel such a poignant connection to the unknown? The touch ignites a conflagration within my soul, an awakening that sears through every fiber of my being. A surge of energy ripples outward from where our skins meet, an electric storm that drowns out the silence of the swamp. My blackened heart hammers against my ribcage, each beat a drumroll that heralds a transformation I cannot escape. The tranquility that once cradled my spirit shatters, leaving a raw and urgent need to understand, to grasp the tendrils of this dark power that binds me to my unearthly kin.

Visions flash before my eyes: cryptic symbols, faces obscured by shadow, battles waged under blood-red moons. Each image imprints itself upon my mind, a tapestry of violence and beauty stitched with threads of dread and wonder. I can taste the metallic tang of fear on my tongue, yet it is laced with the intoxicating spice of destiny calling to me from the depths of time. What am I becoming? What have I always been? The answers lie with them, in the solemn gravity of their gaze, and I am hurtling toward a truth that promises to consume me whole.

The energy that flows between us is an ancient and endless river of stars in the night sky. Their presence, a trio of statuesque elegance in tailored suits, anchors me to this moment. To the left, a huge tall demon, probably around 6 '4, adorned with intricate tattoos peeking through the suit; he has messy midnight black hair and striking black eyes that seem to hold a hint of mischief, which rivals the cheeky smirk upon his face to perfection. To the right is another towering specimen with dirty blonde hair contrasting sharply with his piercing green eyes. Damn, it's like they seem to see right through me. And in the midst of these two, the one my hand has fallen upon, at around 6 '5 he, is a commanding presence of dark brown hair, neatly styled, which complements his dark brown eyes that seem to pierce straight to my soul. Their chiseled features are beautiful and terrifying, graced with red rivulets. Blood drips languidly from the corners of their mouths like crimson tears wept by a mournful moon. The fangs that glint in the dim light are unmistakable tokens of a lineage whispered about in hushed tones and fearful glances, the vampire's heritage.

Terror should grip me, yet all I feel is an overwhelming sense of homecoming. As they kneel before me, the bayou holds its breath, and time bends around us, a tapestry woven with threads of eternity. "Welcome home." They say in chorus, and the words carry the weight of centuries, echoing through my soul.

The End

ABOUT CASSANDRA DOON

Cassandra hates writing about herself in the third person, but here we are. With over 33 novels penned and no signs of stopping, she writes across multiple genres. Unable to be pinned down by just one, you'll find Fantasy, Dark Romance, Young Adult, and even a Detective series in the mix.

Having grown up in a small country town and later lived in the city, Cassandra found a perfect spot she likes to call an 'in-between place'—complete with rolling hills and just a stone's throw from the Gold Coast in Queensland Australia.

While she may have had social media in the past, Cassandra has since declared it's not for her. Her website is now the best place to find out what's happening in her world and to see what upcoming books are on the horizon.

Standalone:

The Kings of Willows Peak

Damaged Goods

Tuesday May

The Devils Cut

The Detectives Mate

Dark Dahlias Rite

A Field of Tulips and Bones

Follow Poppy

To Her

Blood moon

Unit 9

Broken Creek Ranch

The Dead Zone

Eclipsion (Coming Soon)

Oakland Harbour Series:

Missing

Found

Home

The Boys Series

The Boys Of Hastings House

The Boys of Bittersweet College

The Boys of Nightsbane University

The Boys of Winchester U (Coming Soon)

Second Chances Series:

The Waterfall

Wicked Bonds

Writhe (Coming Soon)

The Restaurant (Coming Soon)

Umbravivus Series:

The Lost Kingdom of Umbravivus (Coming Soon)

The Crowned King of Umbravivus (Coming Soon)

The Queen of Umbravivus (Coming Soon)

Butcher and the Witch Series:

Poison is always in the Prettiest Bottle

Candles make Great Alibis

Socials with a Slice of Pie

Also By C.L. Doon

The Rain Dang Detective Series:

Still Waters

Moving Waters (Coming Soon)

Standalone:

Second Chances at The Riverbend Café

Lavender (Coming Soon)

Also By C. Doon

Standalone:

Ravenwood Manor

Phantom Navis

ABOUT WRAITH

Wraith is a *freakin' ghost*.
Drifting through shadows, lingering in moonlight, and
whispering secrets through the walls, Wraith exists in that
delicious space between fear and fascination.
The next time something brushes past you in the dark,
when the air chills and your spine prickles like it's got a
sixth sense… Don't scream. Smile. And say,
"Hello, Wraith."

ALSO BY WRAITH

Standalone:

A Field of Tulips and Bones

Bittersweet Snapdragon

Dark Dahlia Rite

Follow Poppy